DEDICATION

For all those girls who hope for rainbows after storms.

PLAYLIST

I feel like I'm drowning – Two feet

Cold sweat – Tinashe

Slow dancing in the dark – Sora. wav

Blue – Jackson wang

I'm yours – Isabel larosa

In my bed – Sabrina carpenter

Make you feel – Alina baraz

Dandelions – Ruth B.

PROLOGUE

ISABELLA'S POV

"My little hummingbird….. Where are you?", Rafael sang and my heart thundered in my chest. I didn't expect him to return this early. I have been tracking his schedule since a week and the confidence that he won't be at home in next two hours made me plan my escape - by tying the bedsheets together I secured them on the balcony railing. As far as I could see was darkness but it showed me hope to escape. If I couldn't run whole way out tonight, I could at least hide.

Five days since I was kidnapped from the restaurant where I was working by a extremely rich and handsome man. Any other insane girl would kill to take my place but I don't have fantasy of getting kidnapped and falling in love with a freaking kidnapper.

With shivering hands and wobbling legs I gently closed the glass door of the balcony and got under the bed. Thankfully the lights were off and it was just the moon light peaking through the glass door of the balcony. So I shouldn't be visible at least that's what I hoped for. Folding my hands and started praying that Rafael leave this room without searching for me so that I could slowly sneak my way out tonight.

As soon as the door opened, my breathe hitched. Tears rolled down from my eyes thinking the worst possibility of getting caught. Without making a sound I stayed under the bed.

Tick! Tock!

Tick! Tock!

Tick! Tock!

The sound of clock filled my ears along with my pounding heartbeat.

Please go away.....

Please go away.....

I kept saying internally.

"Where are you my little hummingbird?", his voice rang again and my whole body shivered.

"I know you are here", he stated and his voice sounding playful as if he already caught me and that thought made me sweat in extremely cold weather of New York Decembers.

Two more days for Christmas and I should have been working in the cafe and singing on the streets and spend Christmas night with all by myself thinking how I might have celebrated it if my family was alive.

"You know.... you can't escape", he said and I could feel him getting closer to me.

"Come on love, don't try my patience now", he warned and my jaw wobbled as I stopped myself from crying.

"If I find you... you will regret pulling this stunt, I will count three, better you come out or else...", his voice trailed off and I placed my palm on my mouth and teared up silently.

I don't know what was his reason to kidnap me, I don't have a rich dad (*not even a poor dad*) who would pay him, in fact he doesn't look someone who would kidnap for money. Was he a serial killer? I don't doubt. But the way he didn't touch me, he didn't hurt me and left me in the mansion to roam around as if I own the damn place but never allowed to step out of the mansion and his guards who were present here guarding the doors in absence of him made my escape a big no-no possibility. So I decided to leave the reasons behind as they are out of my knowledge and escape this fucking prison and never look back.

"One… two… three", he counted and my heart was in my mouth in fear. I didn't even breathe thinking he might hear it since the silence in the room was deafening. I closed my eyes tight, afraid if I open them I would come face to face with him. Few minutes passed but it felt like hours and then his voice mocked in amusement.

"Caught ya!", he said bending down and I snapped my eyes open, looking straight into my eyes with his electrifying blue eyes making me jump and scream in fear.

"Ahhh!", I screamed when he roughly dragged me out from under the bed holding my red locks and it burned as hell.

"Please let me go, please let me go", I cried trashing in his hold with my hands holding his grip on my hair which he only tightened mercilessly.

"Tsk, tsk, tsk, you pissed me off today my little hummingbird, now you are getting on my nerves with these tears, you do know how much I hate to see tears in your eyes, right?", he stated saying the same words which he said when I was crying on the day he kidnapped me and I cried even more looking into his eyes.

He is much taller than me which made me tilt my head almost back to look into his eyes and he brought me close to himself, the only distance we were separated was our clothes, his black shirt and blue jeans, mine a yellow floral dress among thousands of dresses he bought for me.

"Please let me go, I don't even know who you really are and I swear as long as I remember being orphan, I remember I didn't do something bad to anyone, I couldn't be your wrongdoer then why did you kidnap me?", I choked out without blinking.

"Because I want to keep you with me, near me", he said simply. My eyes widened in disbelief and I stared at him shaking my head.

"Let me go please, I... I don't want to stay here", I said gulping down.

His eyes darkened at my words, next second he wrapped his hand around my neck and pushed me on the wall beside the side table.

"No", he declared with so much anger and my legs started shivering in fear. When I tried to kick him he pressed his body on mine and locked my legs between his making me helpless.

His jaw clenched and he brought his lips close to mine almost touching my lips with his own when he said, "You belong here, with me, you can't leave…. If you try to pull the stunt again, just remember".

"You can hide in this cage but can never escape it my little hummingbird, not until am alive", he said smirking.

Goosebumps rose on my skin at his words and I found myself leaning into his touch, bringing my lips close to his as if am going to kiss him but before our lips met I clenched my jaw hard and slowly took the vase from the table and smacked it against his forehead so hard that his hold on me loosened and he fell on his knees in pain.

"Then die you asshole", I screamed at him and ran out of the mansion as fast as I could without turning back.

Little did I know that this hummingbird would never want to leave his cage one day.

~♫♩♪ ♩♪♫~

CHAPTER ONE

RAFAEL'S POV

"Rafael, my baby, promise me that you will not cry, you will be a strong boy", my mother choked out laying on the hospital bed. I know what's going to happen next and I don't want to witness it. I shook my head. "No, please mom", I begged. My hands are little in her bony hands. She is almost a skeleton with skin on her bones. Once her palms used to be so soft and now it hurts when she tighten her hold on mine but I will let her hurt me like this. If she will be with me, if she holds my hand – I will let her hurt me.

But she tells she is a mom and a mom doesn't hurt her child so she said she is going to send me to a better place and I don't believe.

Is their any better place far away from mom? Even if it is, I wouldn't go, I won't trade her for any better or best place.

"Mom, please don't close your eyes mom", I begged and sobbed when she smiled. She is tired, she was always tired from six months and stopped playing with me like once she used to. "I love you so much my little prince", she cooed and blood oozed from her mouth.

"NO!", I screamed but it sounded far and muffled and suddenly I was not that little seven years boy who was crying clutching his mother's dead body and last time I remember, I was sleeping in the bed but now suddenly…I was in the graveyard. At least that's how everything looked. The hospital was filled with dead bodies, cold and bloody, which sent shivers straight to my spine and my stomach churned in sickness.

This was not supposed to happen, hospital was a place for people to leave healthy and happy with their loved ones, we doctors had power to bring health and happiness back in people's life who walked in our worship space but few unlucky people had to accept the fate god planned for them and their loved ones.

Right now in front of my eyes these people are not lying after accepting the fate god planned for them but instead they accepted the cruelty doctors of this hospital gave them. Being one of those doctors I felt sick. My breathing became hard, I couldn't move, am trapped in between the white walls of the hospital which were painted with blood and when I lifted my hands I saw blood on them.

"Dr.Waldorf, you killed us".

"Dr.Waldorf is a killer".

"We won't forgive you Dr.Waldorf".

SKILLED SMILE

The voices cried in my head. I found myself covering my ears to stop them but they were still there and I screamed, closing my eyes tight I kept screaming.

"No! I am not a killer, I didn't kill you, it's not my fault", I kept saying while breathing heavily.

My chest felt heavy and I heard her voice from behind.

"Of course it's your fault baby, you knew what I could do to achieve my dreams, yet you trust me with people who trusted you".

"You are a killer, you killed them, Rafael".

Her voice made my skin crawl and I gasped for air shaking my head, no, I didn't kill anyone, am a doctor, I save people, I don't kill.

"I am not a killer, I didn't kill them", I screamed so loud and suddenly I am back in my room.

My whole body was sweaty and I was shivering with aftermath of the nightmare which always make me afraid to falling asleep. Running my hands through my thick and sweaty dark black hair I signed catching my breathe.

"Bad dream again?", my best friend Carter asked walking inside my room without having sense to knock. His dark brown hair was styled perfectly and he was wearing his signature black leather jacket and jeans with a white T-shirt underneath.

"Bad memories… I would say", I answered looking for my phone. Two hours of sleep I caught tonight and I would say it was worst since the medicines should have worked for at least six hours. I think the universe is punishing me because one mistake I did – trusting her.

Was that only trust?! No it wasn't, it was love, I was blinded by my love for her and she ruined me – love ruined me, ruined my career, ruined my life. The lavish life am living now keeps reminding me the life I lived few months ago.

"Since you are awake how about we go out and grab drinks in a club and get laid?", Carter asked casually and I nodded my head thinking I would forget about that incident of my life for sometime but I never expected the most bitter part of my past to smack me right on my face in the form of a pretty little red head.

~

"The best part of your club is there is no shortage of women who is into bdsm", I tell taking a sip of fruity and subtle sweet Brandy which has a hint of oak wood flavour since it was perfectly aged – just according to my taste.

"Compliment coming from you is rare doc, so am going to brag about it", Carter tells smiling proudly and I frown.

"Don't call me that", I growl and my friend raise his hands in surrender and smile looking behind me.

When I turned my head to look at what made him smile, a blonde wearing a tight red dress which stopped right below her hips and her boobs plunging out was looking straight at us with her lustful blue eyes.

"Katherine, she is good at it, submissive just as you prefer", my best friend said and I smirked wickedly.

"Enjoy your night", Carter said and walked away on the dance floor to find his own flavour of the night and I chugged the remaining drink in my glass and walked towards the blonde who was looking as a perfect prey and I intend to hunt her taking my own time.

CHAPTER TWO

ISABELLA'S POV

"You should wear the pink dress, it looks good on you", Lisa said looking between the two dresses I held out in front of her to select.

"Right?! I was however saving the red one for Christmas", I grin placing the red floral frock in my cupboard and walked into the attached washroom in my two bedroom apartment which am sharing with Lisa.

The place is pretty much packed and the bathroom is not one would like to spend drinking a glass of wine in the bathtub due to the small space but I won't complain about the first ever place I get to call as my home.

Growing up orphan wasn't something easy, specially when you were thrown in the system at the age of seven. As soon as I turned eighteen I moved out and rented this apartment with Lisa, splitting the bills by working in cafe in the mornings and singing on the streets with our band which I happened to join three years ago.

Wearing the pink floral dress over my white lace lingerie I tied my red curly hair in ponytail and applied nude lipstick and let my freckles be tonight's star.

Getting out of my washroom I saw lisa texting on the phone. "Bruce and Nick are waiting for us in front of the Chinese restaurant", lisa said getting up and looked at me grinning.

"I bet tonight we are going to make lots of money not only with your angelic vocals but your ethereal form too, goddess Isabella", she said bowing in Korean style making me roll my eyes but I ended up smiling at her compliment.

"Come on let's go", I said dragging her out of my room with my guitar and black fur coat and shoved my legs in black knee length boots.

I waited few minutes for lisa to tie her shoe lace and she wore a brown leather jacket over her white button up and blue jeans. Locking our door we excitedly got in the cab to reach our destination.

~

"You look beautiful as always", Bruce said hugging me and I smiled hugging him back. "You look handsome too", I tell and When we broke the hug we saw lisa and Nick eating each other's faces and we both sighed rolling our eyes.

"I think we came here to grab noodles before heading to the time square street?", Bruce asked clearing his throat to grab attention of the love birds.

"Right", I agreed nodding my head and my friends chuckled breaking the kiss and Nick muttered "Jealous asses", under his breathe and I ignored the last part where he whispered to lisa about eating her up for dessert.

I swear to God, I don't want to hear what they are going to do after tonight's show in lisa's bedroom which is right beside mine and the lack of sound proof walls are a freaking punishment.

Planning to hear jazz music with headsets on till I fall asleep I followed my friends in the restaurant with our guitars and keyboards with other electric equipment for busking.

"Oh god these taste amazing", I moan slurping the ramen before having a spoonful of steamy soup.

"Nothing can beat spicy noodles and coke in cold nights", lisa tells and we all agree nodding our heads too busy to talk.

"By the way bella, did you finish the song you were writing?", nick asks wiping his mouth with tissue.

"Not yet, am unable to think past the lines I already wrote, lack of inspiration", I said shrugging my shoulders.

"Promise me, I will be the first person to hear the song when you finish", Bruce asks excited knowing my answer.

"Sure", I tell him giving him a wide smile and we all get back to eat our dinner in peace.

~

"See! I told you", lisa exclaims happily gathering all the money from the donation box and I smile at her widely knowing we made good amount of money.

"I told you what?", nick asks as he put the electric equipment in the car and lisa snakes her arm around my waist and tells, "I said that she would gather a huge audience tonight and dang! our baby did it".

"Shut up! It was our team work", I scold her rolling my eyes not wanting to take all the credit myself and she smiled patting my shoulder and said, "If you insist".

"If you don't want to feel like third wheel between them, how about we go grab a ice cream before I drop you at your place?", Bruce suggested smiling.

"Ohhhhh", both Nick and lisa teased giving each other looks as if Bruce asked me on a date. I sighed internally shaking my head knowing the relationship between bruce and me is only friendship and in fact we are best friends since we both grew up together as his family was neighbours of my foster family.

"Let's go Bruce", I said ignoring them and he put helmet on my head as well as his and we both got on his bike, waving my hand to grinning lisa and nick we drove away.

CHAPTER THREE

RAFAEL'S POV

I like how you can roam care free in New York city, no one gives a fuck about who is walking beside you. As much as I like this, the worst side of the city is traffic. Though after having a great time in the blue house club, am getting frustrated sitting in the backseat of my Rolls – Royce.

It's snowing yet people are out enjoying the midnight life of new York City.

"How much time its gonna take?", I ask my driver and he politely reply.

"It may take thirty to forty minutes, boss", he tells glancing at the road packed with cars.

Groaning internally I turned my head to my left and my eyes widened as soon as they fell on that person. I felt like I couldn't breathe, everything around her turned blurry. All I could see is just her. As much as I want her to be real I know I am seeing things because of drinks I have taken. The red curly haired woman was eating ice cream in fucking freezing winters and she was smiling so wide that it hurt my jaws.

She was standing by the bike joking with a man who was almost my height, his brown hair sprawled on his forehead wanting me to believe that he might be her brother but the way he is watching her, admiring her laughter with those eyes which I once used to have for a particular woman – whom am seeing in *her* tonight.

But she… she seems different, different in a way that it terrified my soul. I fisted my palms hard in rage.

"You are seeing things, rafael, because of the useless sleeping pills you took and mixed them with alcohol".

I reasoned myself trying to stop myself from walking towards her and take her life with my own damn hands. No, this woman is not her, she is dead for good and as truest as it is, I am dead too from inside.

Blaming alcohol I sighed peeling my eyes off the redhead and thankfully the traffic cleared up faster than predicted and my driver drove the car back to my mansion.

SKILLED SMILE

~

As alarm rang I blinked my eyes, another night without sleep. At this point I should stop taking pills. Nothing works for my nightmares. Frustrated, I break the clock throwing it across the room. It immediately stopped working and somehow I felt relief. From past three months I am unable to sleep without falling into the loophole – dreams. In my case these are not dreams but the true incident and I feel more helpless when I get struck in them.

But last night it was something intense because I never imagined things and seeing her as if she was real fucked up my thoughts. I would have believed she was alive if I didn't see her die in front of my own eyes.

But what if she was alive? There were many ways she could have faked her death and fooled me as she kept doing for two fucking years. I need to confirm that it is my imagination and nothing more.

With that thought I got up from my bed which was wrinkle free and went straight into the en suite to take a quick shower. Then I blow dried my hair and wore a black jeans and white shirt, I took a olive green pea coat over it and my eyes fell on my neatly pressed white coats hanging in my walk in closet. The stethoscope placed under them was a reminder what I was.

The news three months ago played in my head as if it's just yesterday.

"Dr. Rafael Waldorf, the famous cardiothoracic surgeon, the gold medallist of Medway university resigned his job at the age of twenty eight, it is believed that it's because of…".

I snapped out of my thoughts and sighed pinching my temple. My head was pounding so hard that I would die if I didn't grab a Americano on my way. Wearing white sneakers I walked out of my mansion towards my destination.

~

"Boss, we have reached new hope church", my driver announced and I took a deep breathe. It's not snowing but the snow from the last night is still covering the footpath and the roof of the church.

There is a corner decorated with flowers and I guessed looking at the guests.

"I think there is a wedding going on, stop the car near the back gate", I ordered and ben nodded his head before telling "yes boss".

In five minutes the car stood in front of the gate and the place itself screamed difference between it and the other side.

"You can go now", I said getting down the car and ben called me back.

"But boss Mr Hawkins said I can't….", I cut him off immediately not wanting to hear what Carter said to my driver – obviously some shit about not leaving me alone anywhere as if I will kill myself.

Why would I do that favour to God when he is already killing me internally? I couldn't save them but he could have but he choose to enjoy the company of people who raised toast of wine in front of him singing some melodic phrases from Bible instead of

SKILLED SMILE

helping or at least sending help to the people who really needed his help.

"Last time I checked, I was your boss", I growled at him and he lowered his head and muttered a "Sorry boss".

Without turning back I walked straight through the gate, my shoes digging in the pile of snow and I felt irritated when my socks felt wet. *I should have wore snow boots.*

Ignoring the feeling I took a shovel from the tools in the store room and walked where she was supposed to be buried.

Passing through many graves which didn't have any roses or cards as it used to be in other seasons I snickered. I think people remember to stop by their loved ones only when the climate is comfortable.

However my reason for coming here wasn't out of love, it's because I hate this bitch so much that I couldn't digest the fact I saw her in someone.

Digging the snow first off the graveyard which has the tomb of her name I cleared the pile of show and found the wet soil, just past this she is inside a black coffin. I turned around to look if someone is around, if they do they would have already called cops telling a crazy man is digging a grave, thought I would be out of the trouble with a single call, it would be a waste of time. Sighing to myself I held the shovel tight in my hands and dug the soil until it hit the coffin. Looking around one last time I exhaled heavily. This is it, if she is here then I indeed should stop mixing up meds and alcohol, if she isn't, am going to find her and kill her with my own hands this time.

My knees were covered in mud as I wiped my hands over my thighs and uncovered the coffin and then my eyes widened, for once I thought my sight betrayed me but no, I stepped inside the empty coffin, it's empty, where I saw people burying her... suddenly she isn't there anymore. Unless if someone dug the grave before me or if she put the show for everyone to believe she was dead when in fact she was alive, happy somewhere after destroying lives of so many people.

With sweaty hands I filled the pit as it was while I clenched my jaw hard. I was angry and frustrated that I was fool enough to trust her, not only once but twice.

But this time I will not trust her and find her wherever she is and give her what she deserves – death, just as those innocent people died, she will die a painful death. The fun part would be that I will kill her with her own medicine just as she killed them.

CHAPTER FOUR

ISABELLA'S POV

"This would be so much fun", I tell giggling as I help lisa to colour her hair just as my natural hair colour.

"If one redhead could make that many dollars, I think two would make a fortune", Lisa tells chuckling and I laugh shaking my head.

"It's amusing that people used to bully me in school for my hair calling me carrot head and gingerbread but when we grow up

SKILLED SMILE

they want to see more redheads", I tell applying the hair dye with the brush as she looked through the mirror in my eyes.

"Do you know why people bully?", she asked and I found myself shrugging.

"It's because they are jealous", she said smiling softly and I exhaled a humourless chuckle.

"I don't think so", I tell and steal my eyes from hers and hold my tears in. It wasn't easy to get bullied every time in your school. My pain didn't end there, I had few friends, at least they claimed to be my friends when all they did was use me for their needs. Asking me to do their assignments and get them things when they lazily sat in their seats. The worst thing was it didn't end there, the foster homes I stayed before they kicked me back in the system which used to search me so called family as soon as possible to have me back again. This kept happening until I was took by my last foster home when I was sixteen and then I met bruce. Honestly that place wasn't any good but bruce made it bearable.

"It's true", lisa fights back and I lose my cool.

"If it was true then why I was bullied for not having parents, obviously people wouldn't have been jealous of me because I don't have them!", I seethe and slam the brush on the table and walk out of her room.

Knowing she will come behind me I immediately put a baggy jeans over my jeggings and fixing my black hoodie over my shirt, I walked out from the apartment after grabbing my backpack.

Wanting to stay alone for some time I walked towards the nearby park. My phone rang and I sighed knowing it's lisa. Though I feel bad for lashing out on her but I couldn't stand when people thinks am some strongest person who went through so much in their life. Specially when they think I can take it. No, I can't.

I am just a normal twenty one year girl who likes to have a shoulder to cry on, a person she could trust her secrets with, someone instead of saying you are strong tell that it's okay, it will be fine, am with you.

Am not asking for pity but am not asking for praises for the shit I went through and people either gives you pity or pat a on your shoulder instead of understanding what you actually want.

As I hoped there weren't much people in the park. The sun was peaking out through the clouds which were storing snow for some other hour and the snow below is melting away slightly making the path slippery.

Thankfully I came wearing anti skid boots so that I could take less stress about landing my ass first on the ice. Sitting on the cold swing I started rocking it mindlessly and sang the song I have written.

I have few scars no one has ever seen

I will let you trace them with your fingertips

The smiles I wear on my lips is fake

Because I believe no one cares

SKILLED SMILE

Will you help me change my view

By pulling me out from the darkness of my room

Will you wipe those invisible tears on my cheeks

Bringing a real smile on my lips

Am tired being strong

Will you be that someone I could lean on

My tears are invisible but my eyes are not nil

I have my love stored in them for you

So that whenever I see you, you see yourself in these

Because you are my love

You are the reason to love....

"Wow! You sing really well miss", someone said from behind me and I almost jumped off the swing. When I turned my head I found a cute little boy who could be between five to six years. His facial features screamed Asian and when he smiled excitedly walking towards me my heart swooned over his cuteness.

"Thank you so much", I said blushing as I noticed the little boy had a company. The old woman smiled at me and I couldn't help but notice how flawless her skin was.

"I'm sorry to disturb you sweetheart, my grandchild wanted to swing and when we came here you were singing so beautifully that we were enchanted to wait till you finish", she said smiling softly and I found myself easing up.

SKILLED SMILE

"No it's okay, I really don't mind", I tell getting up from the swing and offering it to the boy.

"What is your name, little champ?", I ask him helping him to get on it.

"My name is Li jie and am five years old", the little boy tells and I smile widely.

"Your name is beautiful just as you", I compliment and he blushed looking at his shoes while sitting on the swing.

"Should I help you?", I ask and his grandmother hesitated before saying, "No, sweetheart, it's okay, I can take care…".

I smiled cutting her off and started swinging him by standing behind the swing.

"It's okay, I would love to play sometime with li jie", I said and the boy squealed in joy.

"Miss what is your name?", he asked and I chuckled at his cuteness before answering, "Isabella".

"Miss Isabella, I think I am in love with you, will you marry me?", he asked and both me and his grandma burst laughing. Holding my stomach before coming down from my laughing fit, I asked him one simple question.

"Will you bring clouds to me? I love them a lot", the boy immediately nodded his head as if it's a possible request and I swooned over his cuteness and kissed his cheek.

"Then I will marry you".

SKILLED SMILE

CHAPTER FIVE

RAFAEL'S POV

"Then I will marry you".

Her words hung in the air for good few minutes stopping me on my track. I wasn't imagining her, not now, not last night. She is real and alive and when I finally found her I don't know how I should approach her and tell she fucked up really bad.

I followed her, afraid that she will disappear if I blink and stood there really shocked when she started singing, it felt like if she was pouring her soul out but again devil doesn't have a soul. I never knew she could sing and when I thought deeply, does I even know anything about her I could trust?

When I snapped my thoughts back to the reality I took long strides towards her but soon someone stopped me with their hand on my shoulder, then his voice was heard and I didn't turn back.

"What the fuck is wrong with you Rafael?!", my best friend scolded and I simply accepted turning towards him and said looking into his eyes.

"Everything".

He grabbed my arm and hissed, "Why the fuck you were in church, digging up her grave? Have you lost your damn mind?!".

"I saw her, I saw her last night, she is not dead, she is alive", I choke out and Carter's eyes bulged out in shock.

Shaking his head he said, "No, that can't be possible".

"It is in fact I saw her just now, see", I pressed pointing my finger where she is. His frown said everything, snapping my head back to the swing, I groaned fisting my hair.

"I missed her! Shit! Shit!", I screamed kicking the air.

"She must be somewhere around", I started running nearby trying to find her.

"Rafael! Rafael!", Carter yelled following me.

"She must be here", I said running on the snow and almost tripped but the urge to find her didn't stop me.

SKILLED SMILE

After looking around the park entrance I made it clear that she have already left away. And I need to find her at any cost which I don't know where to start from.

~

"Are you sure you saw her?", Carter asked for the nth time and I had to shove down the urge of choking my own best friend. Giving him a look which said 'was I on drugs?' and said, "I'm sure".

"I saw her eating ice cream last night and thought I was hallucinating because we both know how much she hates ice cream and cold weather, yet there she was", I tell taking a sip from the brandy bottle directly.

"First I thought because I mixed meds and alcohol but as the night passed by I understood, that wasn't hallucination", I stated chugging down the drink and Carter snatched the bottle from my hands and I let him have it for once knowing he would need a drink too.

"But didn't we saw her dead body which was in the coffin and the way of her death wasn't something easy that she could have escaped", he points out and I internally wince at how she faked her death.

Falling from the tallest building wasn't a way one could escape their death and how she is alive is literally out of my thinking capacity. If any one could trust me it will be a miracle itself as disbelieving as she is alive sounds. "Well then I guess that bitch can cheat death too", I tell dropping my shoulders.

"I think we should ask his help", Carter tells and I narrow my eyes at him. Am I thinking about the same person he is referring? Then fuck it am never going to ask him for help. Not even when am dying.

"Don't", I warn even before he gets to take his name.

"But Rafael...", I immediately cut him off with a warning.

"If you want to stay alive, you better not mention his fucking name in front of me, not even think about that bastard when you are anywhere near me".

"Then how are we going to find her?", he grunts and I sigh again.

I should have gone for her when she was right in front of me instead of wasting my time on my thoughts. "I have a idea", my friend snaps his fingers excited.

"We will put our men around the area you spotted her, if she was there once, there is a chance of seeing her again".

I nod my head considering the idea, well this is the only best thing I could see when I can't ask around for her and she knows how to fake, we should be more discrete approaching her. Once the fish comes in our net we will smack her hard on the ground.

"I think... it's a good idea", I tell and Carter smiled widely.

"So what is it? Mission finding HLCB?!", He asks and I scowl at his code language.

"HLCB means heartless cheating bitch", he tells Chuckling and I found my self smirking.

SKILLED SMILE

"Baby.... You would be welcomed in my life this time so that I could send you to hell with my own hands".

"Come on let's go, we don't have time to chill around", I tell dragging Carter out of his club.

~

ISABELLA'S POV

"I am sorry, Lisa, I was stupid, I shouldn't have taken my anger on you like this", I whine but she kept ignoring me.

Ugh, how am gonna make her talk to me?!

Stupid Isabella! Idiot Isabella!

Knowing how protective Lisa is of you, you had to walk out on her!

"Take this to table number four", Nick tells handing me the order.

I pout at him eyeing his girlfriend and he raise his hands in surrender.

Hah! Thought he would help you knowing he couldn't stand a chance against his girlfriend!

"Ugh, okay", I tell stomping my feet and take the tray and walk towards the table number four.

Placing the drinks on the table I gave a professional smile to the two men who seemed out of place. Their conversation was halted when I asked, "Do you need anything else sir?".

SKILLED SMILE

"No, you can leave", the man with blond hair replied and I nodded my head but his eyes suddenly fell on me and his expression was as if he have seen a ghost.

I gave a uneasy smile and cleared my throat before taking a step back and the man spoke. "Actually…we need something else, any desserts? What would you suggest?", he asks leaning on the table with a smirk and I gulp visibly shifting uncomfortably under his gaze.

"I… I think vanilla ice creams are better dessert with Americano", I tell stuttering and mentally smack myself.

His eyebrow was pierced and there was a tattoo just above his eyebrow, his two hands covered in various tattoos which were clearly visible in his short sleeve T-shirt. Noticing my eyes on his toned body he smirked again and I mentally wacked myself. He might be thinking I like his body but in fact I was afraid.

Run from here before he hit on you and you panic for straight two hours, you Dumbo.

"Then we will get it, right matt", he asks another dangerous looking man and he smirk and wink at me.

With shaking hands I walk nodding my head with a small smile.

Why they were looking at me as if they know me?

Whatever I will ask Nick to attend the table.

"Two vanilla ice creams at table number four", I tell Lisa and she prepare the order without even looking at me.

SKILLED SMILE

"Nick, can you please attend table number four, I don't feel comfortable around those men, they were giving me weird looks", I ask him whispering so that no one hear us.

"Did they tell something to you?", Nick asks worried and I shake my head before muttering "No".

"It's okay I will take it, stay here", he said leaving me to take care of counter and I sigh smiling.

Thankfully after few minutes those two men left but not before giving me a weird look. I gulped uneasiness and Lisa covered me from their gaze, no matter how mad she is she always care of me. My lips twitched a little but I yelped when she poked her elbow in my rib.

"Don't smile, Isabella, am still mad at you", she scoffed and I pouted giving her my best puppy eyes knowing this would definitely work on her but still she remained still as a stone.

"Okay, I will do anything you tell", I offer knowing I will regret this later.

Sighing heavily a sinister smirk plastered on her face, when she heard my offer.

"Pinkie promise?", she asks and I nod my head hesitating.

"Fine, I forgive you, if and only if you will twin with me for tonight's show", and in that moment I know am going to regret about this my whole life.

"Bella", Nick calls me, his eyebrows furrowed as he approached near us.

"Yes?", I ask him confused.

"Do you know who those men were?", he asks out of no where and I shake my head.

"I don't know who they were, Nick", I tell confidently.

"It's weird because they were telling that you know them and what was the weirdest thing is that they were calling you Annabella", he said and I scowled shaking my head.

"No, it must be some misunderstanding, I really don't know them", I stand on my words.

There is no way that I know someone like those men. Dangerous, shady and wicked. Their aura made me sick to my stomach not that they weren't good looking, they were in a sinful way. Specially the one with eyebrow piercing, he was like black poisonous apple which could make princess from fairy tale fall asleep for ages.

Shivering at the way he looked at me I shoo the thoughts away and sigh. "Let's just get back to work", Lisa suggests sensing my distress.

"Yes, let's get back to work", Nick tells and I move from the counter giving him his place.

The remaining day passed by thinking why they thought I was Annabella, then again they didn't seemed to be trusted so I scolded myself for stressing on it.

~

SKILLED SMILE

"I swear to God! Please Lisa this won't even cover my ass and it's fucking winters", I fight back to not wear the dress Lisa selected for us tonight.

"Hoes don't get cold", she said flipping her red hair back and I smack a pillow on her face and she laughed her ass off looking at me.

"You should have seen your face God! I should have recorded it! That was insane", she huffs between her laughter tears streaming down her face and my lips twitch in a smile knowing she was just messing around me and I am thankful that am not going to wear that hoes don't get cold dress and die before few days of Christmas by freezing my ass.

"You are a bitch", I scoff and she kisses my cheek cheekily and I do a puking sound.

"Yah! I will kiss your lips if you puke off my kisses", she complains and I giggle doing what she asked me to not do.

"You are going to regret it sweetheart", she sang and took me with her on bed and we kicked and punched each other playfully performing all our funny moves on bed and if someone walked in on us, they would definitely think lisa is cheating on Nick with me.

If people don't think you are gay for each other are you even best friends? —

No!

~

Two hours in my room passed as if it were minutes and we ended up wearing matching blue Jeans and blue T-shirts which read 'mentally fucked up'.

I guess that implies for two of us, can't fight on it.

Singing our favourite songs while playing guitar in the NewYork streets when its snowing but not as much as you would want to warm up in your home. That's what I love about winters, it provides cold that you seek warmth and when you do, you automatically melt and so does your worries.

Waiting to go and cuddle my orange teddy bear on my bed I packed up my guitar and handed the cash collected to Bruce.

Today too we made a huge amount and I think it's because of the Christmas season and after the end of winters Bruce wanted us to take auditions but I don't think I would make it. I like singing, I live to sing for the people around me but not for popularity. I believe the more popular you get you leave your comfort behind and I no where in my life want to lose it.

"I will come back in a moment", I said to Lisa and walks pulling the hood of my black hoodie and went towards the nearby cafe to get myself a cheesecake. Lisa is on diet so she won't eat it so I can have all pieces for myself unless Nick steals them from me.

"No matter what keep an eye on your desserts and keep your *two eyes* on *cheesecake*", that's the rule when you live in a shared apartment.

CHAPTER SIX

RAFAEL'S POV

We stayed in the park and took rounds around it, walking through some apartment buildings as a sick stalkers we spent our evening. Knowing it's getting dark and the night life would have already begun since 5pm in the times Square we drove off to the blue house club.

Carter was still doubting that I have indeed seen her but I can't blame him. Looking for his VIP guests he appointed the manager as head of anything happens tonight in his absence and told him to call if someone decided to kill someone in his club after that he waved his hand to his bar and joined me in my car.

I mentally rolled my eyes at his over acting. This bastard doesn't miss his club, he is missing the night he could have if he stayed there but no, me as his one and only best friend he will do anything to help me. Anything in *terms and conditions*.

"You need to give me the mature brandy you were saving for when your mood hits", he tells and I scoff.

"Carter, last time I remember, I bought it from your club and if I have a box of that thing in my home, you have a truck of them", I tell exhaling heavily.

"Well you know how much I like free drinks", he bargains and I tiredly nod my head.

"fine", I tell and he celebrate his victory with a yay! Yes! And my driver barely holds back his laughter. I should have fired him for filling about me to my best friend but with everything going in my head, I don't afford time to get a new driver. Ben was loyal so I gave him a second chance.

"I like how busy it gets in times Square with all the street singers and in fact few street singers are better singers than who earn million and billions on their albums", Carter rants and I let my eyes search for her.

SKILLED SMILE

Better singers – I should agree on this that she sang really well and her voice was just as deep and innocent as the lyrics but then I scoff mentally.

Deep and innocent my foot! If she have anything deep in her is darkness and innocent doesn't stays in the same book where her name is written. That's how she is – a narcissistic psychopathic greedy bitch.

"We need to get down if we want to search for her, we can't find her in this crowd by sitting in the car", I tell and get down from the car and Carter follows me.

The packed busy streets isn't what I like and specially with Carter who isn't missing a chance to enjoy his time looking at the street performers. Fine! I regret bringing him with me but it's out of my hands now. After few long hours we couldn't find anyone with red hair and now I doubt if she have already figured out that I saw her and changed her hair?

"It's going to be midnight, I think we should come another time", Carter says and I found myself nodding my head.

"Let's go", I said getting inside my car. A yawn escaped from Carter's lip and he seemed like he might pass out anytime till we reach home.

Thinking about sleep I winced internally. Turning my head to the right and looking out of the window and the growing snow on the streets I felt a pang in my chest thinking about the times I used to play in snow with my mother when I was a kid. With that memory, the memories I want to push away invaded my mind and I felt a shiver run down my spine.

I wasn't concentrating at what am looking but that hair, bright oranges shade of red and I know it was her.

"Stop the car!", I yelled not blinking my eyes. I didn't even let it stop and got down from it when it slowed down and ran. It didn't took much time to reach the car which was about to get started and I placed my hand on her shoulder and the man with her immediately jumped in between pushing me away. Carter came following me and then I saw her face. Its not her, not the one whom I was looking for but some other girl.

"Nick!", she gasped looking at her angry friend? No, by the way he reacted boyfriend it is.

"Sorry", Carter said slightly distancing me from the Nick guy.

"It…it was a misunderstanding", I force out and they both nod their head. Holding my arm Carter drags me away from them and I grit my teeth.

Now Carter will definitely think am going crazy and seeing things. He won't trust me but surprising me he speaks, "See man! I understand you, I believe you, we need to take things from behind the screen obviously we won't get our hands on that bitch if she watch us before we catch her", he tells and I find myself smiling.

His eyes are puffy and dark circles were visible under them and I was thankful for the concealer I used under mine or else people would have thought it's Halloween season instead of Christmas.

"We will find her!", he tells pumping his fist and I exhale.

"yes, we will find her, soon".

~

"I just want to go to this new restaurant to try out their famous dishes not to hear a bitch talking about herself over food", Carter huffs.

"I said, I don't want to go", I told in a bored tone.

Basically he heard about a restaurant opening and wants to try the food but he wants me to join him. I reminded him that he can take any girl he wants to wine and dine with him but he doesn't want to.

"Please rafael, if I go with you I will get special attention and of course you will be paying", he tells grinning.

I narrow my eyes at him, stopping the workout and wipe my sweat with a towel and he kept chewing on candies he bought this morning. Sometimes I wonder how this man keeps this body while he eats sweets as a girl on her periods!

"Sometimes I wonder you are not real son of your rich dad but a poor boy he took in from the streets", I tell and he frown shaking his head.

"No, I am his own blood, born in a famous hospital and it was even recorded", he tells and I scoff.

"I doubt, old habits die hard brother, I think you indeed were a homeless guy he took in by the way how stingy you are when it comes to money", I tell and he laughs throwing his head back.

"No I am not", he tells and I smirk.

"You want me to come?", I ask and he made a disgusting face before telling.

"Come to the restaurant with me", he states as if I was suggesting something else. I twist my face.

"You are a ass you know that right?", I state scoffing.

"However, I will *accompany* you to the restaurant if you are going to pay for the dinner", I offer and he grins.

"This one time, just to prove you that am not a sting when it comes to money", he tells finally leaving me alone so that I could workout peacefully. Glancing at my sports watch, I guess, I have few hours to shower and relax before going to dinner.

CHAPTER SEVEN

ISABELLA'S POV

Seven days to Christmas.

I crossed the date on the calendar with red marker. From tonight lisa and nick will be spending holidays with their parents and Bruce will be busy with his own. I will be left alone on Christmas like always. Smiling sadly I get into the washroom and take a long warm shower, humming to the jazz music I played on the

SKILLED SMILE

Bluetooth. When I felt skin of my palms getting wrinkled I sighed getting out of the shower.

Everything feels dull not to mention because am feeling lonely. Why does this feeling is so intense? Like I have gone through it for many years but not in this way. Not in a way growing up orphan feels like but in the way of a caged animal. Tied up, helpless in a room with no one around to hear out my scream.

Unconsciously I touched my neck feeling some metal against it and I couldn't breathe. Gasping for air I fell on my knees.

What is happening to me?

"Make sure she doesn't remember anything, I don't want this red bag in my family anymore".

It was a man's voice. He was angry and his words were sounding as if am under the pool. I couldn't breathe again. When I did it hurts but not in my chest or neck but on my forehead. The pain is unbearable it felt like someone is pounding a hammer breaking my skull.

"Help", I cried out.

"I... I can't breathe, please help me", I choked out my whole body was drenched in a layer of sweat. I closed my eyes trying to gain control over my body but all I could feel was more fear. Fear of loneliness, fear of dying in between four white walls.

White walls?! My room was grey colour.

I snapped my eyes open and in shock and fear and I sucked in huge amount of air as I was pulled out from water after staying under it for hours. My phone rang and I walked slowly after getting on my feet. My hands were still shivering when I answered the call.

"Hello bella", Bruce's voice was thick and stressed and there were voices behind him.

"Bruce", I said clearing my throat so that he couldn't hear panic in my voice.

"Bella, can you please come to the restaurant I work, they opened a new chain and it's crowded tonight and we need one more waitress, everyone are on holidays, I know it's too much to ask but can you please make it till tonight?", he asked and his words were hushed.

"It's okay Bruce, I will be there", I said but he spoke again.

"No, not where I work, they need a waitress in the new place, am sending you the address", he said and hung up before even I could speak.

Fine, I guess at least I won't be alone today.

Wearing a casual outfit knowing I would have to change in the clothes they will give since it's a famous restaurant I locked the door of the apartment and went to the address Bruce sent me.

~

The restaurant was beautiful, though beautiful would be a mundane. It's magnificent! I feared if my heels will dirt up the cream marble in which I could see my damn reflection. Long mirrors in the hallway with authentic paintings of naked people I couldn't help but blush. They were so realistic and I appreciate the art and love it. It shows vulnerability and strength in single

SKILLED SMILE

glance and that makes people real and their paintings realistic. Anyways, if the back entrance of the restaurant is this beautiful I couldn't imagine how extraordinary the main hall would be. I spent few more minutes admiring the art waiting for someone to tell me what am supposed to do.

"Miss Miller?", a woman called me and I cleared my throat looking at her. Rubbing my palms on my thighs I gave her a awkward smile. Her eyes scan me for a quick second and she twist her face making me gulp nervously. "You need to get dressed ASAP, we can't let someone dressed up like you seen in our restaurant", she snapped before turning.

I bit my tongue to stop myself from saying something. Am doing this for Bruce, I reminded myself and when she asked me to follow her I quickly did. "Wear them", she said handing me a bag and I quickly opened it to find a short black skirt and white shirt with black bow for collar. I bit my lip nervously as she watched me with a raised eyebrow.

"Ahem, sorry but isn't it a bit short?", I ask chewing my lip and she rolls her eyes.

"Wear it and meet me in kitchen, we are too busy to measure the skirt", she said and walked out and my jaw dropped open.

What the fuck does she think?!

Clutching the bag tightly in my hand I take my anger out on air, I punch it, kick it, scream at it then get dressed.

If uncomfortable was a face, it would be this dress. It's loose on my waist, tight on my ass that I am afraid it will tear off if I bend.

And shirt – well let's not talk about it. Basically this uniform look less of a restaurant waitress dress more of a sex club stripper uniform. I think we should award the person who designed it with – world's best *runaway dress* award. As these clothes make you want to run away from the job which provide it as damn uniforms.

"Here, attend table number three", a man said handing me the menu card and I found myself nodding and fix my posture and pull my skirt down which kept riding up and I ushered myself where am needed.

~

The night went by really well and I managed to not tear my skirt off and keep my dignity. Well at least that's what I thought until I attended new customers. They looked as if they were drunk, ignoring it I simply got down to my work.

"May I take your order sir?", I ask the group of four men and one of them looks at me while licking his lips with a sinister smile which made me shift uncomfortably from my one leg to another.

"You can take anything from us, sweetheart", he said and I internally cursed.

Here we go

SKILLED SMILE

Ughh Oh god! Lowering my skirt which kept riding up I pressed a smile and stated, "When you are ready to order please tell me".

The other three men gave a look to the one who was smirking and thankfully he stopped from talking further and they placed their order.

Holding the tray in one hand I walked towards the table and I felt something come in between my way and tripped and fell down, face first taking the tray with me.

"Oh my god!", I gasped in pain and fear and the person who was smirking came to me and held my arms trying to look as if helping me but in reality he was the one who put his leg in my way so that I mess up.

"Don't touch me!", I hiss slapping his hands off me.

"You know what will happen if I complain to your manager?", he asks amused and I frown looking at him.

"I will tell it's you who did this", I snap and his smirk only gets wider.

"Hmm, so I will tell that you tried to get into my pants and you damn very well know that it's not new a waitress in a slutty dress wants to suck a rich man's dick", he said smirking and his friends chuckled as if he cracked a joke.

I felt my anger buzzing in my veins and I clenched my jaw hard and I did what any other girl would have done. Slapped him hard on his cheek and it boomed in the hall. Many were already looking at us and now I even caught attention of the manager.

She widened her eyes and rushed towards me but before she could the man raised his hand to slap me back.

"You bitch..", his words and his hand stopped in the mid way as another man held his wrist in a tight hold and applied pressure on it and his face twisted in pain.

"Tsk, tsk, tsk, keep your hands to yourself when they are this delicate", he taunted and threw it off and manager came looking at me in pity. I thought she would lash on me or scold me but she surprised me when she asked, "Are you okay, Miss Miller?".

I smiled at her softly nodding my head assuring her that am fine and winced when my lip stung a little. "Your lip is bleeding", the man with electric blue eyes said and wiped his thumb on my injury and I held my breathe.

"Let's get you cleaned up, you are covered in food", he offered and I felt my head nodding. As he guided me to the staff room he held my hand and I felt warmth spread throughout my body in a humming calmness.

"We don't tolerate this behaviour towards our staff, you and your friends can leave before we call cops on you for misbehaving", she scolds and the man dare to talk back. "But she...", she cut him off immediately.

"We have cctv cameras every corner of this restaurant", she snapped stopping him off guard.

SKILLED SMILE

Then their voices faded as we moved away from them. "Thank you so much", I said looking at his ethereal face. He has a face of angel, silky jet black hair which was styled neatly, his blue suit was flaw less just as him. His well trimmed beard was so perfect, not a single hair in or out of line. His lips pink and perfect.

He was tall enough that I have to look up at him to meet his eyes with mine and I am short enough that I would break my nose with his chest if I run into him.

I licked my lips unconsciously and his lips twitched then suddenly his face turned sinister that I regret comparing him to an angel and smirking wickedly he just covered my face with his large palm and I couldn't scream. His arm tightened around my waist when I kept fighting him with all my might but this fucker turned out to have demon's strength. He dragged me out of the restaurant into a car which was right near the door and my eyes widened as I realized I was getting kidnapped and with last hope of someone finding me before this man chop me in pieces and feed them to sharks in the ocean, my eyes shut as darkness consumed me because lack of oxygen.

CHAPTER EIGHT

RAFAEL'S POV

I couldn't believe my eyes when I found her. I knew I wasn't hallucinating and this time Carter saw her too and he turned pale as if he saw a ghost. Understandable low-key I felt same. Because seeing the rich, spoiled brat like Annabella Davis as a waitress and defending her self respect instead of taking room number of the men who hit on her was quite amusing. I waited, waited to see how she would react but slapping him shook me and Carter.

At that moment I sensed that bastard would raise his hand on her I immediately sprint towards them and though I was talking to him, my eyes were on her. She wasn't afraid, wasn't surprised, she was just thankful?! Yes, almost happy that someone was there for her. Her fiery orange red hair was in tiny natural curls unlike what she used to have before – Blonde straight hair.

Still no matter what she made me go through this stupid heart still cared for her when I saw her lip bleeding. Unaware of my own action I wiped the blood from the corner of her lips. A blush painted her face as she blinked at me in surprise and I offered to help her but little did she knows my true intentions.

When I held her hand, her aura was different than she used to have before. Not mysteriously inviting but innocently baiting. I will kill myself, if I let my heart fall in the same pit. Scoffing internally at the stupidity of my heart thinking how am comparing the same person with herself as if they are as different as sun and moon. This woman might be putting the facade but I know the dirt within her soul which makes my skin crawl and this time I will rip her mask one by one until she tells me the reason for playing with innocent people's life.

Though she may mask away her other intentions her lust sprouts out clearly and I smile knowing I have same effect on her but unlucky her I have something else planned for her. My face expressed my true intentions and her face changed from

SKILLED SMILE

admiration to shock then paled when she realised am a no knight in shining armour but a devil in disguise for her.

~

"I still can't believe it's her, can I... can I touch her to confirm?", Carter asks looking at me through the rear view mirror. Thankfully we didn't bring driver with us tonight as Carter decided to bring his car. I glared at him and he cleared his throat and concentrated on driving us to my mansion safely.

Sighing to myself I looked at her at her passed out state. Her features look relaxed and I could see faint freckles on her skin. I didn't wonder if these were fake because I know they are, just like her now brown eyes instead of light grey and her dyed red hair.

I clenched my jaw hard in anger as my palms were fisted on each side of my thighs.

"What we are going to do with her now?", Carter asked looking straight on the road.

"I have a plan", I tell and take my phone out from my pocket.

"Hello, yes Anastasia, I want you to open the guestroom and Mark will come to fix cctv camera in the room in ten minutes, tell him I told to not put one in en-suite", I ordered and she replied with "Okay boss".

"Drive to my pool house", I tell and I watched carter's eyes bulged out of his eye sockets through the rear mirror.

"No way you are going to held her hostage!", he exclaimed throwing his hand in air and I smirked.

"Not just held her in hostage, leave her all alone for few days before asking her what we need to know", I tell and carter frowned.

"And what? You think she would spill everything just like that?!", he scoffs and my smirk widened.

"Of course she will, if she wants to get out from her biggest fear", I said shrugging my shoulders.

"Biggest fear?", Carter asks and I confirm.

"Yes, Annabella's biggest fear is staying locked in a room... alone, even if it's just for few minutes", I revealed and his eyes widened but the next words from him made me frown.

"But what if she isn't Annabella?", he asked and I wasn't going to consider it as a possibility.

CHAPTER NINE

RAFAEL'S POV

Sitting in the office of my pool house I waited for Annabella to wake up. It's been an hour she was off, if my guess is right she should wake up any second now. I asked Anastasia to change her clothes and now the woman whom I hate most in the world is sleeping under my roof in *my* shirt.

Iconic.

Pouring myself a drink I chugged whole glass in a single gulp. Exhaling heavily I massaged my forehead closing my eyes for a second and when I opened Annabella was stirring. Stretching her body as a cat she rubbed her eyes with heels of her palms and looked around her surrounding with a frown. Still asleep and confused she sat on the bed pushing the duvet off her body and stood on her legs.

"Where the fuck I am?!", she gasped and her voice came out raspy. Rubbing her sore throat she looked at the glass of water on the bedside table and slowly walked towards it and picked it up as she examined her surroundings.

Smelling the water with a scowl on her face she sighed and it almost made me laugh.

Thought I would kill you this easily?!

Drinking a glass of water hastily she sighed in content and then her eyes drifted to her clothes.

"Oh my god! Did that asshole rape me?!", she gasped and removed few top buttons of my shirt she was wearing and examined her body.

I would die poking myself with needles instead of touching you bitch!

I scoffed when she sighed again understanding that she was unharmed in that way.

Slowly she walked towards the door and peeked through the keyhole. Trying to open it she grunted and explored the room, the balcony sliders were locked. She couldn't escape from en-suite.

After realizing she was locked in a room completely alone I thought she would freak out any second now but the little minx went back to the bed folded her legs under her ass and sat comfortably chewing her nails.

She is stressed.

I scowled looking at her again, Annabella used to keep pacing in a room if she was stressed but... I waited for few more minutes to let her show any signs of panic attack she used to get but no, an hour passed and she didn't panic but started singing.

The night is cold

Am all alone

Sitting on a bed

Waiting for love

Time is getting old

You haven't shown

Am now losing all my hope

Don't...leave...me...walking away from...me

I couldn't live without you, without your love...

Her voice was melodic, mesmerising better than what I have ever heard in my life. It's….It's angelic which will melt your heart in a second and bloom a garden full of flowers in it. But then she stopped singing and a lone tear slipped out from her eyes as she cried.

"I don't think I will be able to finish writing this song and sing it to you Bruce, am sorry for not keeping my promise", she choked and I felt a stab in my chest.

Bruce? Is it the same man with whom she was laughing with when I first saw her. Who was looking at her with so much love that made me sick to my stomach.

She cried again and this time big fat tears spilled out of her doe eyes and her breathing was getting heavy. She covered her face with her palms and brought her knees to her chest and welled. With her every cry I felt my heart bleed and when my eyes fell on her under thigh near the seam of her panties my eyes widened.

No! How is this possible?! As much as I remember Annabella should have a deep gash on her thigh which was stitched but now it feels like it was not even there. Not believing my own eyes I zoomed, Carter walking in on me and calling me pervert was my least concern as I stared at the screen intently.

I shook my head in disbelief, my hands turned sweaty and I zoomed back at her face. Slowly removing hands from her face she wiped her tears which kept flooding through her brown bambi eyes which were turned red. Her makeup must be long gone now and what I saw instead of clear skin made me curse.

Her nose and cheek bones were covered with beautiful freckles, not less nor more just enough to decorate her flushed skin. Her nose were reddened because of crying and the way she was rubbing her eyes there is no way there are lens in them.

As realization drawled in my head I felt as I couldn't breathe. I kidnapped someone innocent who exactly looks like Annabella and what's twisted was that am not guilty but hurt. Hurt because she was crying and an urge to wipe her tears embraced me. I couldn't see her cry nor imagine her singing for someone else. I want to see her laugh with me, smile at me and I groaned punching books off from my desk.

I am going sick in my fucking head! What the hell is wrong with me?! I groaned pulling my hair and exhaled before taking a deep breathe. Her cries echoed again and this time I couldn't stop myself from staying away. I hastened my way towards the guest room, I unlocked the door using my finger print and the door opened wide.

She yelped and jumped in her place and her hand flew to her chest. She sobbed with her eyes closed and her face turned redder than before as she saw me. Shaking her head vigorously she cried, "Please don't sell me to anyone".

I frowned looking at her with my hands in my trousers pockets. "Why do you think am going to sell you?", I asked amusement slipping in my tone.

She stopped crying and opened her one eye and looked at me before opening another and hugged herself tightly before answering to my question.

"Because I have seen in movies, mafia men kidnap young women and sell them to old perverts to get richer", she tells and I fight back a smile.

"Do I look like a mafia to you?", I ask and she furrow her eyebrows and stare at my face then my body to my shoes. Looking into my eyes she answers, "yes, you look like a mafia".

I didn't stop my smile this time and her eyes widened for a second watching me smile and blushed looking away. "Well, sorry to disappoint you my little hummingbird, am a doctor", I tell and she snapped her head towards me and her mouth opened wide in shock.

"Oh my god", she gasped, her lips quivered and she cried her wiped her runny nose with *my shirt's* sleeve and asked, "So you are going to sell my organs after killing me or will you take my organs out one by one until I die?".

"Are you always like this or you went in shock after getting kidnapped?", I ask and she bite her lip looking at me with her teary doe eyes.

"Aren't you a doctor? You should figure out if I got a mental trauma after getting kidnapped you asshole!", she yelled getting up from the bed.

Her feral features were a fucking turn on for a man like me who feast on making woman submit and I smirked at her fuelling her anger. "I swear to God! Whatever you are doctor, mafia, teacher, I don't care let me go!", she said pushing me and when her palms touched my torso I sucked in air.

"No, you aren't going anywhere my little hummingbird", I said pushing her wild straw hair behind her ear and she slapped my hand away.

"Don't touch me", she seethed as a wild cat and I raised my hands up in air respecting her decision.

"Please, please let me go, I swear to God, I won't tell to anyone about this", she tells while straightening my shirt on her thighs. It's almost near her knees so the reason to rub her hands isn't for covering herself. She is stressed? No, she isn't.

Then what could this be?

Thinking?!

Yes, she is thinking a way to escape, indulging in talk she is seeking time and the way she is walking towards me – she came close so she could escape as soon as she gets a chance through the door behind me.

Her eyes looked behind me time to time as she tries to keep my eyes on her.

"Hummingbird, my eyes will always be on you as a eagle keeps its eyes on its prey".

I kept a cold face and looked at her as I spoke. "What is your name, hummingbird?"

"Ughh! Don't call me that!", she growled coming more closer and I internally smirked.

"Then tell me your name Miss Miller", I state poking my tongue in my cheek knowing am getting on her nerves.

SKILLED SMILE

"You kidnapped me even without knowing my damn name?!", she grunted throwing her hands in air dramatically.

I smirked, "Mistakes happen and I swear to God, kidnapping you was the best mistake I ever did", I said shrugging my shoulders.

She narrowed her eyes on me and clenched her jaw and one last time her brown eyes shifted from my blue ones to the door and she sprung towards it but I caught her with my arm around her waist. "Leave me you leaping lizard!", she cursed trashing in my arms and I smiled dragging her towards the bed. Her back was pressed on me making me lose my every last ounce of patience.

"You bloody tarter sauce! leave me!", she choked welling tears.

Turning her around to face me I slowly pushed her on the bed and hovered her tiny figure. Her eyes were tightly closed and tears were escaping them stabbing my heart

No matter how badly I wanted to kiss her tears away but I didn't. Instead I hushed her then spoke.

"I don't like to see tears in yours eyes hummingbird".

Slowly she opened her eyes and our faces were so close that one single movement and we would kiss but she turned her face aside after looking into my eyes with a unexplainable expression and answered.

"Isabella, Isabella Miller".

CHAPTER TEN

RAFAEL'S POV

"So we kidnapped a wrong girl?!", Carter asked pouring himself *corn flakes in the milk*. Am not judging him for it. It's his food *which I bought* of course and it's his choice.

"Yes, her name is Isabella Miller and as far as I know Annabella Davis doesn't have any relatives with the name Miller", I tell looking at the email my detective sent me.

There is a picture of her in a floral frock with her three friends and another one in a waitress uniform serving in a cafe. Luckily he could collect these from the cctv cameras of places she works. Days in cafe and nights on streets singing.

Hmm, no doubt she can sing so well.

"Her date of birth is different too", I tell reading her details out loud for him to hear.

"She is twenty one, birthday January eleven, nothing much about parents – both were dead in a car accident when she was seven and…", I halted my words when I read it.

My heart dropped in my stomach, gulping the uneasiness of that place. Carter's expression frowned when he asked, "What's wrong rafael?".

Without giving him a eye contact I still kept my eyes on the email and said, "She… she was in the same orphanage as mine but..".

"But I never saw her there", I revealed looking into his eyes.

~

ISABELLA'S POV

"Who are you?", I ask groggily when someone knocks the door. Door? I can't even figure out where the door was. Everything around me is white just plain, bright white and I sat in a corner clutching my floral frock which my mom bought for me for my birthday. Fearing that if I

touch something in this room, I will break or get something dirty and he will punish me. I don't want to get punished, it hurts so much.

"Eden, my name is Eden", he tells and I smile politely forgetting he couldn't see me.

I wipe my tears but they still flow. This time I didn't bother to stop them and cried. I don't know why? But I just felt like to cry a lot as if am mourning someone's loss.

"Why are you crying? Who are you?", he asked.

"I'm... am... I don't remember my name, am crying because I have been punished", I tell sobbing.

"Punished? Can I know why?", he asked again and this time his words were sounding sad.

My mom would be just as sad as him when I tell her this bad man is punishing me.

"Bec.. because I was a bad girl and I... I... I ate chocolate", I tell and there was a silence and I felt him shuffle something before the sounds disappeared.

"Don't cry, please", he cooed and I saw a chocolate beside me.

Oh I was sitting against the door?!

"Here, eat this chocolate", he said and my hands almost reached out for it but I remembered how that bad man will punish me when he will find about this.

Pushing the chocolate back from the gap underneath the door I shook my head though he couldn't see. "I can't eat chocolate or else I will be

SKILLED SMILE

punished", I tell and he just waits for few minutes before pushing it back.

"No one will punish you, eat it now, and give me the wrapper back, I will cover up for you, am here", he said and I smiled doing as he said.

"Thank you Eden", I said and he asked.

"How old are you?".

"I'm seven years", I said and he hummed.

"How old are you Eden?", I asked and replied.

"I'm fourteen".

"Fourteen, you are bigger than me, Eden, can you please take me out of this room, am afraid", I pleaded.

I was waiting for his answer, waiting for him to say yes, yes - he can take me out from this room. The brightness surrounding me disappeared in one blink, I stood right in the middle of the room and was screaming. But a single hand pulled me on the chair and my hands and ankles were tied to it. I know how much it pains, no, I don't want to get punished, I didn't do anything.

Eden! Eden! Save me!

Eden!

Eden!!!!

"Eden", I screamed out of my lungs and gasped for air, I rolled over on the bed until I fell down with a thud. The pain didn't bother me. I rushed towards the door. Crawling and sobbing as I was gasping for air.

"Help me!", I cried as I slowly placed my hand on the door knob and someone opened the door. It was like a dream come true. I was always trapped in my nightmares sometimes I don't see them, sometimes I see them and fear is the only feeling that crawls under my skin when I see them and I couldn't peel it off.

"Miss Isabella!", a woman said wrapping her arms around me.

"Are you okay?", she asked worry and fear dripping in her voice but my ears were ringing and I couldn't speak because of the lump I feel in my throat.

Hitting my chest twice I cried and then she hugged me rubbing my back in a motherly way.

"Shh, you are okay, no one is going to hurt you", she cooed and I felt myself relaxing a little.

Am not alone, am not alone.

I kept repeating in my head as I took a deep breathe and the barrier I thought I have in my throat disappeared slowly.

"I'm… am okay now", I said my voice came out cracked and the woman hummed breaking the hug.

"Let's get you some water and food", she said helping me stand up.

SKILLED SMILE

"I made your favourite breakfast", she said surprising me.

"It's already morning?", I gasped and she nodded her head smiling faintly.

"These are your clothes", she said opening a door and revealing a walk in closet filled with many floral frocks and midi skirts and shirt to cardigans, jeans and jackets, not to mention hoodies too. My eyes widened as I saw lingerie section and the whole place looks like it's filled with life time necessities.

Hah! As if I will let him keep me here forever, I will escape from this place as soon as I get chance. No one can cage me, am not a bird at least not a *hummingbird*.

I clenched my teeth and took a simple ankle length blue frock which is shoulder less and a white cardigan to wear over the dress and simple black lingerie and walked inside the en-suite to shower.

Talking about how huge and well kept this bathroom is will hurt my ego and am not going to tell it's beautiful and I can spend hours in the Jacuzzi, but no, as I said, I won't tell.

Rolling my eyes at the expensive female skincare collection I just grabbed a body wash and shampoo and took shower after brushing my teeth. After getting dressed I Blow-dried my hair and thought the woman would have brought my breakfast in my room but surprisingly she guided me to a hall. I was looking keenly all the routes and made a mental note of every door on which my eyes fell.

So I was on the second floor, there was another and the ground floor which has a open dining area and living room connected together. The lady pointed towards the door and said it was kitchen but my eyes were glued to the main door which was larger than any other doors I have seen.

The place was decorated with greys and white with some gold and black aesthetic decorations all over the place and a hint of blue which made everything look perfect. Blue... just as I thought about the colour, a pair of blue eyes looked at me intently and the owner of those azure eyes walked towards me standing straight in front of me with his hands tucked in his pockets.

I stepped back, because of the closeness he looked as if he was hovering me. With that the thought of him on me last night invaded my mind and I felt my face heating up but thankful for winters it won't look as if he was effecting me.

His sharp jaws were more visible as he was clean shaved unlike the first time we met. But his eyes, his under eyes were puffy as if he didn't sleep.

I frowned as he spoke, "You can go anywhere you want in the home, Anastasia will give you a tour after breakfast and don't try to escape, the building is surrounded by guards", he said and turned his back to me and walked out of the main door as if he ordered his new pet and I just gawked at him until the lady who's name is supposed to be anastasia chuckled.

I scowled at her biting my lower lip not understanding her reason to laugh.

SKILLED SMILE

"You were looking at him like you are mad he didn't give you a good bye kiss", she spilled out and my eyes widened and I shook my head so fast that I almost saw stars.

"No! It's not like that, I was looking at him as someone who got kidnapped glare at their kidnapper", I retorted and her features saddened and she changed the topic.

"I hope you like pasta, since you didn't eat anything last night I thought to make the breakfast heavy", she said before placing some dishes and plates on the dining table. "You should finish when its still hot", she smiled politely and for a second I thought to protest. But not wanting to embarrass myself with a growling stomach I sighed and got on a chair and savoured the pasta as if it's my last meal and who knows it could be when you are living with a kidnapper.

CHAPTER ELEVEN

SKILLED SMILE

RAFAEL'S POV

Five days since I kidnapped Isabella. No single day passed without her throwing a tantrum over not wanting to eat something and when no one watched she slowly crawled out of the bed and ate up the food as a good little girl. I didn't keep an eye on her from the cctv once I confirmed that she wasn't Annabella on the first night. So I put anastasia to tell me anything to everything she was doing. My little hummingbird was so mad that she denied for a house tour but her eyes always pinned the main entrance which she thinks she could escape from there one day.

But she is underestimating the trained guards who are surrounding the place if she is thinking she could escape and in their absence which is when am at home, it's impossible because I am always wide awake the whole night and in the living room, bar having drinks.

I was busy with filling my hospital with newest equipment required for treatments. Its been a busy week since I have to stay there for dealings and donations of old machines with few new ones in the hospitals in rural areas where people could get minimum of the facilities possibly they get in cities.

Anastasia is trying her best to get along with Isabella but Isabella put a line in between them realizing she won't be any help for her to escape my cage. My little hummingbird was getting impatient to leave me but I don't intend to let her fly away from me.

SKILLED SMILE

My personal detective gathered some more information about Isabella and her friends and they are still oblivious about where she was. Saying Isabella didn't feel well I took off from the restaurant and the manager didn't protest knowing how I came for her rescue. Bruce...well he texted once and twice and I texted him back with her phone and threw the phone away.

Walking in the hall where press meeting is going to start in few minutes all I could think about is Isabella and nothing else. What she would have been doing? Probably singing, I cursed myself internally remembering the effect of her melodic voice on me. I sighed heavily as paparazzi started taking pictures and shoving cameras and mics in my face. Thankfully my bodyguards made a way for me to reach the table placed on the stage which was covered with a clean white cloth and with water bottles as well as few decorative flower bouquets which were given by some not so important women with cards in them which had their phone numbers written with a thirsty texts. Would I look like bragging if I tell some of them even dropped their room numbers?! Anyways.

Ignoring them completely I made eye contact with every reporter sitting in front of me with their mics placed on the table.

My PR gave them a green light to ask questions and here we go.

"It's been three long months since you made your presence in media Dr. Waldorf, how does it feel?", a reporter asked and I pressed my lips together before answering.

"To be honest, I don't like to be a talk in the media but I wouldn't be able to promote new medications and it's techniques if I didn't face the camera, I wouldn't mind if it's only for professional reasons, I don't like public's interest in my personal life", I answer and my PR, Varun Malhotra gave me a nod of appreciation with my pleasing answer.

He is known for his best work in clearing up the damaged image of business men, celebrities, sports persons and what not. He was appointed this job of clearing my image from the accident happened three months ago. That wasn't even my fault if it was – I just trusted a wrong person who not only ruined my professional image but my soul too.

"Dr. Waldorf, how do you keep up to date with medicine and trends?", a journalist asked and I gave him a impressed nod for asking something useful question instead of digging my personal life.

"Medicine and trend may not seem related to each other with usage of traditional meds and procedure of treatment but they do in a discreet way, medicinal revolution always brings up a new medical trend".

"My personal opinion on this connection is one should always be interested in a medicine and it's usage minding the side effects which may differ from person to person, I would never advice people to go with trend neglecting the professional advice which may be dangerous to them but perfectly fine for others".

"And one can easily get their hands on these at nearby professionals and internet plays a huge role, just as you all, I keep myself updated with internet but never put that in usage unless I get the background theory and it's side effects and efficiency of the medicine with professional help", I answer and hear a multiple impressed oh's and ah's from the audience.

My PR grins and claps which caused others to clap following him and I internally roll my eyes while my hands are fisted underneath the table.

"Dr.Waldorf, we have heard that you donated all the old equipment along with few latest ones in the rural areas, is this because its your way trying to make people forget about the horrific incident happened in your hospital?", a female journalist asks and I glare at her. Rolling her stray hair with a pencil she chews the chewing gum smirking and my PR who was sitting beside me tried to interrupt but I stopped him.

"Actually, No, it's not my way to make people forget about the tragic accident, am doing this since I started studying medicine, then I used to provide free health camps as charity and now when I can afford whatever I want I am providing equipment which aren't available in reach of financially challenged people", I said and another round of claps echoed in the hall.

I saw the female journalist clench her jaw then she spoke again. This time she definitely poked my sore wound.

"How did you cope up and moved on from Dr. Robert Davis's grand daughter?", her voice was taunting as if she knows she pulled the trigger. Her smirk said everything that she is here not to appreciate my work but to pull a reaction out of me trying to prove that I could be behind those innocent people's deaths in my hospital. Sticking to what my PR recommended I pulled a straight face and answered looking straight into her eyes.

"She was my professor's granddaughter, nothing more, so it wasn't hard for me but she shouldn't have killed herself and should have faced the consequences of her mistake".

"But Dr. Waldorf there were rumours about you both dating and also that you are behind her death as well as those thirty seven innocent cancer patients…", I slammed my palms on the table loudly getting up from my seat.

"I didn't date her nor I was involved in that incident, my vaccine was perfect, someone swapped it and I believe it's Annabella and she killed herself before we caught her and it's none of your business whom I date", I snapped at her and she flinched

SKILLED SMILE

because of my harsh tone. My PR immediately grabbed my arm but I slapped his hand away.

"Meeting dismissed", he announced and the bodyguards started surrounding me and I angrily walked out of the hall from the back door when others exited from the common exit area.

"I told to keep your cool, Dr. Waldorf, we can't bring your chit clean...", my PR halted his words when I glared at him coldly as if he speaks one more word and I will snap his neck without thinking twice.

Leaving him behind I got in my car and turned on my laptop. It's a long way journey to the pool house so deciding to watch the live footage of my hummingbird's room watching her pulling a little stunt of tying the bedsheets to the railing of the balcony so that she could escape. I smirked and ordered my driver, "Drive fast to the pool house".

CHAPTER TWELVE

RAFAEL'S POV

I wasn't mad seeing her try to escape, I was just amused with her idea. Does she think she can get down the second floor hanging down a DIY rope she made out of bedsheets?!

I called Amanda and asked her to leave as well as the guards as I was just few minutes away from the home. Isabella's eyes stayed on watch all the time. Her hands shivering in fear and cold, she isn't wearing her cardigan. At this rate she is going to be sick. Clicking my tongue I turned my laptop off and the car stopped at its destination.

"You can leave now, I will be staying home for few days", I said earning a "Okay boss", from ben.

As soon as I stepped inside the pool house I sighed. Winters are getting harsh this year. I made a mental note to send warm clothes to the orphanages.

Suddenly there was silent everywhere, I guess my hummingbird realized I am back home early. Walking on the staircase I saw few doors open. I almost chuckled, she thought I will be wasting my time to check on the rooms she messed up as if someone robbed. Even if I don't know it was her trap I would have still gone behind her because she is my treasure and I intend to keep my treasure safe even if it would cost my life.

"My little hummingbird…. Where are you?", I drawled entering into the dark room. My eyes scanned the place which was Illuminated with the moon light from the balcony.

For a reason I know where she hid herself and I smirk playing her game. If my hummingbird wants to play hide and seek her hawk will pretend he didn't see.

Walking towards the couch my shoes made sound with my every step and I could hear faint breathing of Isabella from under the bed.

Just where I thought she is.

"Where are you my little hummingbird?", I called again and this time my voice came out taunting, knowing where she was and I could practically hear her heartbeat echoing in her chest.

"I know you are here", I said smirking.

"You know you can't escape", I mocked her and this time I felt anger towards her for trying this.

She shouldn't have thought about leaving me, she can't leave me. What would have happened if I didn't saw, she could have fallen from the balcony and hurt herself badly, she would have lost in woods in this cold. A shiver ran down my spine thinking about her getting hurt.

"Come on love, don't try my patience now", I warn her so that she come out by herself and drop the fight to run. But no, she didn't.

My jaw clenched at her bratty behaviour.

Anger seeped under my skin and I strolled towards the bed.

"If I find you… you will regret pulling this stunt, I will count three, better you come out or else.…", I warned clenching my teeth. Giving her one last chance to accept her fate. She is destined to be mine, *my hummingbird is destined to be in my cage.*

"One… two… three", I count taking time between each number hoping she comes out and I don't have to cut her wings.

She stayed under the bed and I smirked wickedly, I guess it's time to teach a lesson. Taking my time I slowly bent down and there was she, with her eyes closed, her red locks sprawling on her forehead, her lower lip between her teeth chewing it mercilessly, hands fisted in fear but she was so determined to not come out.

Impressed with her will power to do what she wants instead of accepting defeat knowing she has no chance to win I smiled but then it turned into a smirk and I mocked, "Caught ya".

Her eyes snapped open and she jumped in fear as a scream erupted from the core of her throat. Smirking I caught her red curly hair in my fist and pulled her out from under the bed.

"Please let me go, please let me go", she cried trashing in my hold but I tightened it not letting her free. Her face was stained with tears and fresh tears fell from her doe eyes cracking my heart.

"Tsk, tsk, tsk, you pissed me off today my little hummingbird, now you are getting on my nerves with these tears, you do know how much I hate to see tears in your eyes, right?", I asked her and she cried more closing her eyes.

I brought her body close to mine and she gazed up with her teary eyes. My tall height made her look at me with her neck tilted back and I pushed the desire to possess her pink tortured lips.

"Please let me go, I don't even know who you really are and I swear as long as I remember being orphan, I remember I didn't do something bad to anyone, I couldn't be your wrongdoer then why did you kidnap me?", she choked out without blinking as she looked in my eyes.

I clenched my jaw and thought, why am keeping her with me? Why I want her around me? Why do I feel good to have her in front of my sight? Those thoughts rushed in my head and I poked my tongue in my cheek and said, "Because I want to keep you with me, near me", I stated and her eyes widened and she shook her head in denial.

"Let me go please, I... I don't want to stay here", she said gulping down and I felt a pang in my chest hearing her.

My eyes darkened at her words, very next second I wrapped my hand around her neck and pushed her on the wall beside the bed side table.

She gasped at the impact and teared up but I was so blinded in my anger.

"No", I declared with my harsh tone and she started shivering in fear. If fears keeps her near me, then so it is. But then she tried to kick me, not allowing her I pressed my body on her and caged her in between my legs.

My jaw clenched and I brought my lips close to hers almost touching them when I spoke, "You belong here, with me, you can't leave…. If you try to pull the stunt again, just remember". I said breathing in her scent.

"You can hide in this cage but can never escape it my little hummingbird, not until am alive", I stated smirking.

Her eyes widened and she gulped relaxing in my touch I found her leaning into my touch, bringing her lips close to mine as if she is going to kiss me and I relaxed. Looking into her glossy eyes I gulped and next second I found something hard hit my forehead and I winced in pain falling on my knees.

Fuck!

"Then die you asshole", she screamed at me and ran out of the room as fast as she could and dark spots formed in my sight as I looked at her with blurry eye sight hoping she doesn't get lost in the woods or die in cold weather on her way to reach help and by the way I was still thinking about her safety I know – I am *obsessed* with her. Little did I know this obsession will turn into

SKILLED SMILE

love and one day I will be breaking every single damn cage of the world to make sure my little hummingbird fly high throughout her life.

CHAPTER THIRTEEN

ISABELLA'S POV

I didn't bother to turn around to see if Rafael was dead or alive, I just hope I didn't hit him so hard that next morning I see cops knocking on my door. I didn't even think about the cold weather outside and ran in my slippers and dress without a coat. The cold air stung my skin and I shivered but the fear of getting caught was so high that my blood turned colder than the temperature if possible and I began to run on the narrow road. The slippery road thankfully was covered with ankle depth fresh thick snow and I worked on my legs running in my highest speed. I sniffed with my blocked nose and I realized I couldn't breathe. I sucked air through my mouth and I felt soreness in my nasal cavity. I bet am turned red due to the cold temperature but I didn't accept defeat, not yet.

I ran few more meters till I couldn't see anything clearly with my heavy blurred eyes. My feet turned numb just as my fingers and I felt my body burning with cold till the core of my bones. My teeth were shattering and I felt my lungs heavy and tight and a unfamiliar sting in my chest. My speed eventually slowed down as I stopped in my track falling on my knees. Taking a good look around my surroundings I blinked my heavy eyes. I saw pitch black darkness, the sky was darkest shade too, killing every single possible sight of moonlight. From what I could figure out , I was in the forest. This *physchomedicpath* kept me in a deep forest?!

My heart eventually started thumping slow and loud that I could hear it ringing in my ears. I thought I would be dead right there but a candle of hope lit in my heart when I saw two headlights of a car. Too weak to stand up I raised my arms and waved them in air and cracked a "Help".

"Please, help me", I cried again and my voice came out ragged. Kneeling in the middle of a road at night isn't a best way to ask lift when you have zero idea about the driver actually seeing you and pulling brakes before it's too late and they run their vehicle over your body.

As the car rushed towards me in it's highest speed my life ran as a reel in front of my eyes. That sad smile of my father and tears of my mom when she kissed me last time, my friends Bruce, Nick and Lisa..... But what surprised me was I also saw a white room without any door and a weird looking chair which sent shivers to my spine. I couldn't blink nor breathe as I stared at nothing. The car skid in front of me with a screech and snow specked my face but I didn't blink. The man who was driving the car got down and cursed under his breathe when he stood in front of me with his car's headlights illuminating our faces.

When I saw the same tattooed man from the cafe who had eyebrow and lip piercing my eyes widened and my body welcomed darkness numbing my brain.

RAFAEL'S POV

I woke up wincing from a pounding headache. My hand immediately found the sore spot of my forehead and I groaned getting up from the floor. Sitting on the bed I cradled my head in my hands recollecting the incidents happened before I was knocked out.

Fuck! I shouldn't have underestimated her. She must have been planning it since long as the way she was determined with now or never with her escape plan. My eyes widened as I realized she ran away, she ran out in a fucking snowfall and God knows how she is right now as it's already more than an hour.

I hastened my steps and reached the main door which was left open and when I stepped out of the home after taking car keys to drive my eyebrows furrowed.

A red Ferrari drove in my compound and I very well know who is the fucking owner of that car. My jaw clenched in anger as my hold on the car key tightened and I glared at the owner of the car who smirked at me sliding his window down.

"Devout doc, such a pleasure to meet you", his voice was filled with playfulness and I clenched my jaw.

"What the fuck are you doing here?!", I snapped at him and his smirk only widened as he enjoys getting on my nerves.

"Well, this isn't a way you say hello to your favourite patient", he annoyingly mentioned our not so pleasant relationship.

"Fuck off! I don't have time for you", I spat at him and walked towards my car but his next words made me halt my steps and I turned back looking at him with disbelief.

"If you are going for finding a red head girl, wearing a floral frock and slippers who could possibly be dead with hypothermia….. Then, no you don't need to go because she is right in the backseat of my car – unconscious".

I didn't wait for a second and rushed towards the backseat of his car and opened the damn door and saw Isabella laying on it looking dead. My heart dismayed at her sight, I checked her pulse and it was faint but there and I immediately sprung into action hoping she makes through it and carried her inside with my uninvited guest tagging us behind.

"I will be waiting here if you need something", he offered but I just shook my head, with a frown on my face I spoke.

"I don't need anything, you can leave now".

"Call me after you take care of her Rafael, it's important", he stated and this time there was no playfulness in his voice but he sounded dead serious.

Placing Isabella on my bed I looked at him, his face serious and his concerned gaze on Isabella made me scowl. "I will call you, you can leave now", I said too busy to waste my time on him but I would be lying if I said I didn't felt gratitude towards him for bringing Isabella to me. God knows in which state she was in when he found her and not to mention the time would have taken to find her and her condition would have worsened in the

SKILLED SMILE

mean time. But he doesn't need to know it so I didn't express instead kept a cold face.

With a single nod he left without turning back and I sighed. Her clothes were wet and her heartbeat was still faint. First thing I did was taking her clothes off and tucked her in duvet and increased the temperature of the room and went inside the en-suite taking off my shirt and put a hand towel under the running hot water of tap enough to bring warmness but not burn.

Checking it on my skin first then walked out of the en-suite and wiped the warm towel on her body and tried my best to ignore her ethereal form. Taking off her inner garments I gulped and did what was necessary instead of feeding my lustful demons.

When her body temperature was normal externally I tucked her back in the duvet after pulling my comfortable oversized hoodie over her which covered almost her knees stirring under the duvet she sighed and found a comfortable position to sleep and I smiled in relief. Making a cup of hot chocolate I brought it near her lips after lifting her head up so that she could gulp easily.

"Come on sweetheart, drink up", I whispered and she tiredly opened her eyes and gazed at me.

Her eyes stayed on mine then travelled down to my lips and I gulped as she licked her lips. Looking back into my eyes she whispered, "You are handsome".

My lips twitched and I nudged the cup towards her lips after blowing. "You need to drink up to keep yourself warm from inside", I requested and she sighed before drinking the delicious warmness and sighed in content at the sweetness which I made sure is according to her taste as Anastasia said Isabella prefer extra sweet hot chocolate.

After she drank more than half cup she denied the rest and I didn't force knowing she should feel comfortable right now. No matter how mad I was on her for running away and not to mention the fear which crawled in every fucking cell of my body knowing she could have been dead if he didn't brought her back in time, pressing a kiss on her forehead I laid her back on bed and she closed her eyes sighing without saying a word.

Mentally making a note to ask why the fuck he was driving towards my pool house I sighed taking my phone and closed my bedroom door behind me gently and called the person I least wanted to have anything to do with.

He answered the call in two rings and I asked, "What does Italy's mafia boss's son – Giovanni Salvatore have something important to talk with a surgeon?".

CHAPTER FOURTEEN

RAFAEL'S POV

"No, Rafael, As a friend once you helped saving his mother's life, I have something important to tell you", he said grimly and I found myself addled.

"What is it Giovanni?", I ask him this time smoothly. I don't know much about him but he is Italian mafia boss's illegitimate son and Giovanni hates his dad so much that he wants to take his position but he loves his mother so much that he couldn't kill love of her life. I didn't knew about this earlier when he called me multiple times for his treatments when I was in my training years but I found out last year, when his mother was admitted in my hospital.

Taking a deep breathe Giovanni said, "Someone put a hit on your girl".

"My girl?", I thought out loud a frown painting my face and he snorted.

"Not Annabella, Isabella, the pretty little red head whom you held hostage even after knowing she wasn't the person you were thinking she was".

His words were sharp and without a doubt which made me clench my jaw. Was he keeping eyes on me? What I do and not is none of his business.

"So you were taking perks of being a mafia's son? Don't you!? Since when you are keeping your eyes on my every fucking move giovanni?", I snapped keeping myself together.

This fucker even had audacity to chuckle on my face. Which made me angrier than before. "I wasn't keeping an eye on you rafael, I just happened to cross my path with her in a cafe and she seemed clueless about me when she saw me, obviously I was curious if she have lost her memory as you doctors tells in movies, but no! Surprisingly she is a different person and if am not wrong you have met her before, in the orphanage, don't you remember it *Rafael Eden Waldorf* or do you need details of what your orphanage was doing behind the social service curtains they pulled in front of public eyes?".

My whole body froze at his words and I felt a rage crawling up on my skin, burning my every bit of patience to hang the phone up and threw it on a wall but he wasn't wrong, he is right and I should have thought about the possibility. She could have been from those kids... another wave of nausea washed over me and I found myself leaning on the door and slowly falling down.

SKILLED SMILE

Gulping hardly I looked beside me and I was back in the time, exactly where my memories brought me.

~

"Who are you?", the beautiful melodic voice bloomed from behind the door.

"You forgot me rockstar?", I asked her with a sad smile.

"I'm sorry, I don't remember anything ", she said on the verge of tears and her voice cracked.

I put my hand on the door hoping I could pass this wall between us someday and wipe her tears. She is just a kid and my heart pained for her.

"Here, I brought your favourite chocolates", I tell passing her a chocolate which I bought from my lunch money. As always she pushed the chocolates back from under the door and I could practically see her shaking her head.

"I can't eat chocolates, he will hurt me", she said and I exhaled in pity for this little soul. She was diagnosed with a obsessive compulsive disorder which makes her harm herself as well as others.

There are many rooms here and said they all have different patients like her who are getting help and that's what a fourteen year old me believed. But in reality they were experimenting drugs on these kids and it was too late until this came out.

"Always remember rock star, the greater your storm, the brighter your rainbow", I said before passing the chocolates back.

This time she pushed half of them back to me and said, "A advice giver should also be a advice taker".

I frowned, I am not going through any storm. She spoke again and this time her voice contained smile. "I remember you, Eden, you are my rainbow".

I smiled, "I'm I?".

"Yes, if this storm passed away, I would like to see you", she said and my heart clenched knowing it won't be possible.

Clenching the chocolate in my hand I asked, "Why".

"Because you are my only friend, Eden, you are my rainbow after the storm", she admitted and a lone tear escaped from my eyes.

Am sorry, rockstar, I won't be here to see you but I hope one day I could see you singing on a stage as a rockstar just as you wished.

~

"Are you listening Rafael?", giovanni asked snapping me out of my thoughts.

I exhaled heavily and answered after clearing my throat, "I will take care of her".

"I know", he said sighing.

"Giovanni…", I halted him before he hung up the call.

"Yeah?", he asked and I found myself asking.

SKILLED SMILE

"Annabella... she isn't dead, I didn't find her dead body where it should be, can you...?", I hesitated but he spoke.

"That bitch! Don't worry, I will keep my men on it".

"Thank you", I said feeling gratitude towards him. For not only bringing Isabella back to me but also hinting she could be one among those twenty kids who were..... If she was one among them, it's a miracle she was alive. I should ask her? May be not now, I guess it would be better finding it from a private detective.

"No worries bro, take care the danger might be lurking just near your shadows", he warned before hanging up.

Sighing to myself I shoved the phone in my pocket and fisted my hair frustrated. Deciding to grab a drink knowing I won't be able to sleep I walked towards the bar in the hall and poured myself a drink before turning the laptop on and put on headsets. Playing the cctv footage of Isabella's room from the first day I sipped my drink but when she rolled down the bed screaming my name the hair on the back of my neck stood and my breathe hastened. Eden, that's what my mother used to call me telling it's meaning is place of pleasure and delight and she found it in being a mother to me, in me.

I don't know why the hell I introduced myself as Eden to my Isabella when I couldn't bring her out of misery knowing very well that I could have brought her from that hell which she went through.

SKILLED SMILE

And when it's confirmed that she was indeed my rockstar then how is she normal and alive when others who was experimented died after losing their minimum energy to lift a spoon, losing all the hair and became a practically living dead bodies who could only breathe?

CHAPTER FIFTEEN

ISABELLA'S POV

"You are my rainbow, Eden", I said and my voice was muffled.

"And you are my rockstar", Eden said and I smiled.

"You are going to help me to get out of this place? I don't like here, it hurts", I tell playing with the wrapper.

"Eden?", I asked again and this time there wasn't any answer.

"Eden? Are you there?", I asked raising my voice.

The wrappers in my hand fell down on the white marble floor and I placed my palms on the door and banged them on it.

"Eden? Please, don't go", I cried while banging my fists harder on the door.

"Eden......", I choked when I didn't hear anything but deadly silence.

Sweat formed on my temple and I took a deep breathe. No, am alone, he will hurt me, no one can save me from him.

I fell on my knees and cried in my palms. The door clicked open and I know who it was. My whole body shivered in fear and I lift my head and saw the same man with my blurry vision. I forgot how to breathe when a cheshire grin spread on his face. Slowly I lowered my head and saw the chocolate wrappers as well as a half finished chocolate. Running my tongue on my suddenly dry lips I shuddered.

"You thought you won't be punished today?", he laughed in amusement when I sobbed in fear.

"Little girl, today is the last day you are getting punished here", he said and I found myself struggling to breathe.

"Because tomorrow, you will be set free for few days before you are brought back to the hell", he said and turned the switch on of the chair and I cried ugly.

"Please don't", I screamed but that man dragged me mercilessly.

"Eden!!!!!!!!!", I cried this time and next second I know was my hands and legs were getting cuffed to the chair and cables were attached to my forehead and wrists and I couldn't scream as a piece of wood was shoved into my mouth as it was holding me to not bite my tongue when the machine was turned on.

A wicked laugh echoed in the room and I struggled as my whole body shook and a deadly ear piercing cry left from my mouth.

"EDEN!!!!!!!", I screamed trashing on the bed.

"EDEN!", I cried screaming, getting down from the bed. The door was opened and Rafael engulfed me in a tight hug, his face pale and he was smelling like alcohol.

"Eden...", I choked out clinging onto him as my life depends on it. "Eden left me, he left me", I cried out and he exhaled heavily his muscles tightened under my touch as I whispered in his hold. Gently holding my face in his palms he wiped my tears looking straight into my eyes with a pained expression.

"Shhh, I won't leave you again.....my rockstar", he cooed and his eyes glistened or I might have seen wrong because of tears in my eyes blurring my sight.

"I won't leave you", he whispered pressing a kiss on my forehead and I signed closing my eyes holding onto him.

This time I didn't fight in his arms and I don't know why..... Why I was calling for Eden and who was he? I always get these nightmares from time to time and why Rafael calling me rockstar gave me peace... a secure feeling? With lot of questions in my head I drifted into inviting darkness.

~

Slowly opening my eyes I sighed when a beam of sunlight kissed my face. It feels like it's been so long since I saw sunlight with cold weather and being locked in this house. A smile spread on my lips until I realized someone's arms are wrapped around my waist.

SKILLED SMILE

I gulped hard nervously then turned around and my breathe hitched finding Rafael sleeping beside me with holding me in his arms.

His dark black hair sprawled all over his forehead covering his eyes. His straight nose and strong, sharp chiselled jaw made me gulp. There is no word to praise his magnificent beauty and I wouldn't doubt – I would have fell for him if we were in different circumstances.

Though the bitter feeling in my heart for him, there is also a place I don't know I could have thought to give someone, is it because the connection I felt with him as I always felt in my dreams?

I almost laughed at the thought, there is no way dreams come true and honestly I don't want my dreams to come true because those aren't some you would like to experience in your life not even in your dreams.

Sighing to myself I slowly push his jet black hair away and his blue eyes peered into mine and I slightly gasped. He was looking intently at me which made me squirm in his hold. He didn't loosen but instead he tightened his hold expecting my next move to get off from the bed.

Groggily in his sleepy voice he said, "Good morning my little hummingbird".

I clenched my jaw and struggled in his hold and a lone tear escaped from my eyes when I understood I was helpless in his hold.

"Please, let me go", I cried and his eyes twitched in anger. I sucked in huge amount of air when he flipped me on my back and hovered over me with his hands holding my wrists above my head pressing them on the bed and I cried.

"Please", I begged once again but he smirked coming close to my ear and whispered.

"You begging me when you are under me is doing me things you wouldn't want me to do.....yet", he whispered sending shivers to my spine.

"I...don't want to be here, you said kidnapping me was a mistake", I try to convince him but he hums before telling.

"I said the mistake I don't regret".

My jaw dropped open and I looked at him in disbelief while tears were streaming down my eyes with frustration.

"Mistakes should be corrected, Rafael", I grit out and he smirks now looking into my eyes.

"Well, I don't usually make one and I specially want to embrace this one", he said and I shoved him off me but he simply looked at me with amusement in his eyes at my failed attempts.

"Asshole, get off me", I gritted out glaring at him still pushing his rock hard chest off me.

"I don't want to", he said and his voice was all playful which made me grit my teeth again.

This man here thinking it's fun to kidnap someone!?

"Why? I want to go back to my normal life, I think you want that too, don't you?!", I ask my hands resting on his chest as I peer

SKILLED SMILE

into his azure eyes, he looks like well slept, he doesn't have the dark circles which he usually cover with concealer.

"Nope, I don't want to get back to my normal life", he said without missing a beat and I gaped at him when he asked….. No, declared the next words.

"Be my girlfriend".

CHAPTER SIXTEEN

RAFAEL'S POV

I said what I meant. I want this woman lying beneath me to be my girlfriend, to be mine in any fucking possible ways. There is no way am letting her go. Why? The same question lingered in my head just as in hers.

With wide doe eyes, bed hair and parted pouty pink lips she gaped at me in disbelief and I didn't blink my eyes. Looking straight into her dark brown eyes I tried to look as casual as I could pushing away the thought how would those lips would

SKILLED SMILE

look wrapped around my cock, how would her beautiful voice will sound fucking ecstatic screaming my name when I fuck her hard….. Just at those thoughts my already hard cock twitched and swallowed the urge to groan.

Last night something ignited in me, fuck! Long before that night when I laid my eyes on her standing with that cheap loser I know there is something in her which kept me captivated just as I held her as my captive but the difference is – I don't want to be free from her as she wants to be from me.

"Why?", she asked and her voice breathless and confused as much as she sounded shocked.

Why? That's what even I couldn't figure out sweetheart.

"Do… do you love me?", she asked and her eyebrows frowned and I asked the same question to myself.

Do I love her? There is no doubt I like her, something about her is intriguing… she is like a mystery book which reveals secrets with every page turned and I don't want to put this book down until I have read and understood every single line, word to the damn alphabet.

But why? The urge to keep her close to me, to want her to myself and fear of losing her… this isn't love, I know because after my past experience I know I couldn't love.

Looking into her doe eyes I replied, "I'm fucking obsessed with you my little hummingbird".

Her eyes widened as she took my words in, analysing and understanding that I meant what I said. Looking into my eyes with disbelief and anger she clenched her jaw and I smirked knowing there is no going back. I am obsessed with her. I want her at any cost even if she reminds me of my most painful memory.

"You are fucking crazy! You asshole, you dumbass cockroach, you idiotic stale cheesecake!", she spilled those words as if they are unpleasant curse words and I laughed nuzzling my face in her neck and her body froze when mine rumbled with laughter.

Her heart started beating fast against my chest and her skin warmed up as goose bumps peppered her skin. I smiled, I couldn't help knowing my effect on her and whispered in her ear.

"Is this a way to tell me I have bad breathe and you love me as you love cheesecake, hummingbird?".

I heard her gasp and felt her shake her head and I detached myself off her and looked into her eyes as she struggled to speak. Opening and closing her mouth thinking about right words she could come up with she just groaned and snapped covering her face.

"You don't have bad breathe and I don't love you".

I don't know why but last line stung like a bitch. Biting back the urge to tell something not so pleasant, I questioned, "Why?".

Uncovering her face she gaped at me and snapped, "How can I love you when I know nothing about you?!".

I nodded my head biting my lip and my brain came up with a solution immediately.

Getting off her I pushed my hair back flexing my tensed muscles, "Get ready, we are going on a date", I announced smiling at her and she got off bed as fast as if any girl would if she saw a lizard in it.

"What's wrong with you?! Don't you understand simple language? I want to go away from you! Not on a date with you!", she exclaimed madly walking towards me and I shrugged my shoulders.

"We are going out so that you can get to know me, though I would tell there isn't much and now don't talk shit wasting our time, get dressed if you don't want to go like this on our first date", I said conclusively leaving no gap for protest and she groaned stomping her leg stubbornly.

I know she would try something stupid like last time so I warn her more like threaten her. Pushing her red wild curls off her shoulder I brushed my fingers on her cheek and said, "If you want your friends safe…. You won't try to run away from me".

Through her gritted teeth she snapped, "Don't you dare hurt my friends".

I smirked, "You think that low of me hummingbird? Huh?..... No, I wouldn't hurt or kill them, someone else will, I just have to ring a call".

SKILLED SMILE

As those words settled between us, I traced her plump lips with my thumb and she turned her to the left side away from my touch. Again it stung but I masked the hurt because she deserves to show she is mad on me when I literally kidnapped her and now forcing her to be my girlfriend.

It's okay, it will take time and eventually things will get better between us. I told myself and cleared my throat and backed off with my hands up in air as she silently teared up.

"Get ready ASAP", saying that I left my room letting her to get herself together and do as I said. Calling my PR I said, "I hope it's not a problem if I go to Paris with my girlfriend for Christmas holidays".

"Dr Waldorf, you have a girlfriend?!", varun gasped and I rolled my eyes.

"We could use your relationship to build back…", cutting him off I warned.

"Nope, we aren't using my personal life to build my professional name, it's up to the people if they want to work with my chain, I don't have to force them until people aren't dying helplessly in my hospital".

Sighing to himself he spoke again, "You are taking your private jet right?".

"Yes and I want it to be personal, seriously personal", I added not because I don't want to get spotted with lookalike of Annabella, because I want it to be special and without media interference spoiling something that will be special to Isabella

SKILLED SMILE   98

and making her feel *special* is something which is *important* to me that I could do it every now and next second of my life.

CHAPTER SEVENTEEN

ISABELLA'S POV

Frustrated, angry, mad, helpless and tired I did what I could. I sat back in rafael's private jet and started eating desserts available on board. Why? Because am mad!

I glared at Rafael who kept a poker face and twisted my lips at him before shoving fork into the cheesecake imagining it as him and took a rough bite of it and a smile broke on his face and I groaned in anger throwing the plate at him.

Lucky bastard was blessed with spider man reflexes as he dodged the plate and desserts which should have smacked right on his face and he did dare laugh at my face and I screamed internally.

"Don't act like a brat, hummingbird", he stated now sitting beside me and I chewed my inner cheek not wanting to entertain him any further.

"Where the fuck you are taking me now?!", I asked him fixing my shawl.

"Can't wait to find out rockstar?", he asked and I frowned.

"Why are you calling me that? My name is Isabella", I snapped too tired of him giving me nicknames.

"So you prefer hummingbird over rockstar? Huh?", he questioned smirking at the point I didn't corrected him when he called me hummingbird and did when he called me rockstar and I fought back the urge to punch his pretty face.

"I prefer you to get the fuck out of my life", I bit back glaring at him.

Suddenly he hovered over me placing his hands on the arm rest of the seat am sitting on and his lips was so close to mine that I feared to move. His minty breathe fanned on my cheek and my heartbeat rose at the closeness. I sucked in a breathe when he licked the side of my lips and I parted my mouth involuntary in a low gasp.

SKILLED SMILE

"Hmmm", he hummed as he looked into my wide eyes and smiled.

"Rainbows always shows up after every storm, hummingbird and I am not only your rainbow as well as your storm", he said looking at me intently and a lone tear escaped my eyes.

"Rainbow?", I questioned and he wiped the tear that slid off my eyes as I gaped at him.

"Rainbow and storm", he whispered and I blinked at him.

"Why?", I asked and he smiled before telling.

"You don't have to wait for storms to finish to see the rainbow, I will be with you in the storms as well as after it", he said and I winced at similar faint memory from my dream.

"Eden?", I asked as my hand slowly made it's own way on his cheek and he froze for a second then leaned into my touch giving me a sad smile.

"I'm sorry rockstar, I couldn't save you", he said and I sobbed ugly as I slapped him across his face and he looked down.

"How dare you use my nightmares and make me believe my nightmares are real!", I screamed at him standing on my legs as I pushed him back.

"How dare you!", I screamed again and this time he looked at me as if I grew any horns. My whole body rumbled at a unfamiliar feeling and I struggled for air. As I looked at him angrily and his eyes showed anything but fear and concern. When he took a step towards me I snapped, "St....Stay away from me".

"STAY AWAY FROM ME!", I screamed as my mind was going back at certain place I used to see in my nightmares.

I gasped for air hitting my chest but I couldn't. I opened my mouth to breathe but I hear sobbing and painful screams of a girl. Closing my ears I looked at rafael who was attentively looking at me as if he was afraid to take a step close to me but worried at my state and wanted to help me and I cried.

In next second he stormed towards me in three long strides and wrapped his arms around me protectively and whispered, "It's okay, you are safe, Isabella".

He kept telling the same thing again and again but I shook my head unable to get rid of the image in my head as I kept sobbing. "Shhh, relax, try to relax sweetheart and take a deep breath", he told gently and I gasped for air but my lungs felt heavy and I couldn't breathe.

"Think about something beautiful, anything, someone you love, someone who loves you", he pleaded and I looked up at him totally freaking out and shook my head.

I don't have something beautiful to think about, I don't have anyone who loves me and the one whom I had - I forgot how they look and do I love someone? If I do I shouldn't have forgotten. Am a failure, am a failure….

I wanted to tell all these but my words died in my throat when I heard that voice in my head.

"You are a failed project, you are a failure".

My eyes widened and I slowly blinked my eyes looking at rafael who's face was looking pale as if he is the one who is hurt. My surroundings started changing into the bright white walls and my hold on rafael tightened.

I peered into his blue eyes then his lips, then back to his electric blue eyes as I stood on my toes and he held me close to him thankfully as I wrapped my arms around his neck and brought my lips close to his. Once again looking into his eyes I blinked and slowly let our lips meet. Kissing him once and twice without any experience. I felt his breathe getting heavy as his hold on my waist tightened. I felt this wrong since I was using him but as much as am guilty I also need this distraction. I need to breathe and pushing away my morals I used the person I should stay away and closed my eyes giving myself into the kiss.

CHAPTER EIGHTEEN

RAFAEL'S POV

Looking her breaking down in front of me, I couldn't think straight. I couldn't gut the fact that this happened because of me, am guilty for her pain, am reason for her sorrow, her every tear and I would do anything if I can take her out of this. Her blood sample I sent was still getting worked out by the best of my team

SKILLED SMILE

and they said it would take few more days for her blood results to come and I don't give a fuck about it until and unless she is safe.

When she cried I couldn't keep myself away from her even she asked me. When I held her in my arms my whole body shook internally feeling her pain, her agony and I was helpless in front of her mind. She should control herself, her mind which is tricking her and all I could do is only help her with words right now in absence of meds which would soothe her.

Then she peered into my eyes and they held hope which mine lack. Her red locks sprawled on her face and her nose and cheeks were red. If it was any other normal time I would have admired her beauty. Her eyes dropped on my lips then on my eyes and I understood what she might be thinking and I froze. She wants to kiss me. Isabella wants to kiss me. The woman who looks exactly like the one whom I kissed so many times… just to be left out with lies, just to be shoved a knife in my back as well as in my heart.

I sucked air filling my lungs with it as her lips met mine and they moved on my lips awkwardly and the only thought invaded my mind was – she never kissed anyone and that makes me the first man. Blood rushed in my cock and I felt getting hard just with a simple kiss and I realized this is nothing like the one I had with Annabella. Her kisses were different than Isabella's. This kiss was sweeter, innocent yet passionate most importantly it was truthful. Isabella was vulnerable and she oozed her vulnerability through the kiss and I wanted to take that away. I held her waist tightly as I brought her closer to myself as if there was any space left between us and deepened the kiss when she closed her eyes. Fresh tears dropped on her face mixing up in the kiss but I was fucked up to mind anything odds about the kiss. She might have thought this was needed to calm herself and she would be regretting this later and scream at herself for kissing me but I don't give a fuck. I am ready to be used by her if I am the only one who gets to see her like this, weak and vulnerable only in my arms only in my cage. Our breathes fastened and I bit her lower lip gently and she gasped opening her mouth for me and I explored it as a mad man who is hungry since ages.

The bulge in my pants was obviously making this hard for me to control but I won't take this further than this. Not now, not like this because even I might be a sick bastard wanting to hold her in my cage, I want her to accept me with her open arms. Hoping to see that day soon, I broke the kiss pressing my forehead on her and she still pressed her eyes shut embarrassed about how she was kissing her kidnapper few seconds ago. I didn't speak neither did she for few minutes which felt like long ass years and I wiped away her tears pressing a kiss on her puffed eyes and she sighed heavily opening her eyes to look into mine and I could practically see her kicking herself in her thoughts with her eyes open.

"I'm sorry, I didn't mean to", was the words escaped from her mouth breaking the silence.

"I….. I just…. Am sorry", she whispered taking a step back and I felt a sting in my heart but I understand what she is going through right now.

SKILLED SMILE

Hiding away the hurt, understanding her pain I nodded my head and she ran inside the suite in my private jet and I sighed sitting down on the seat and held her shawl in my hands. How did this happen? I wasn't able to bring myself to kiss women with whom I fucked but how the hell I kissed the lookalike woman who hurt me the most? But when I thought in depth I know, I kissed her because she wasn't Annabella nor someone like Annabella.

A faint smile spread on my lips as I stared at the cheesecake she ate and involuntary my fingers went up to lips tracing them remembering the feeling of her lips on them. Licking them I found that they tastes like the cheesecake she ate and my cock twitched at the thought of tasting her more in many ways. Groaning internally I signalled staff to clean up the mess and went into the suite to check if Isabella is asleep and thankfully she was. Brushing off her hair off her face I tucked her in a duvet and pressed my lips on her forehead one last time before going into the washroom to take care of the problem she left me with.

~

ISABELLA'S POV

"Where are we?", I asked as I found standing in front of the stairs which led down the plane and I already spotted few cars ready for us and I winced at how shiny and awfully pretty they are. Rubbing my hands together I hugged myself feeling somewhat better in the outfit which I found on the bed when I woke up. The jeans is comfortable and perfectly fitting while the hoodie was warm and cosy.

"Put the hood on, hummingbird, we don't want you catching cold", Rafael said as he did it himself and I frowned.

"Don't tell me you brought me to Antarctica", I snapped rolling my eyes but his next words made my eyes widened and my jaw almost dropped on the floor.

"Okay, I won't", he said casually and I thought he said truth until a cheeky smile broke on his face and I scoffed.

"I wish I had a lot of apples in my life", I commented and the air hostess beside us giggled.

Rafael smirked as he retorted, "There is no apple in this world that is keeping this doctor away from you, hummingbird".

In the blink of my eyes he took me in his arms in bridal style and I yelped in embarrassment when everyone around was seeing us as if we are the newly wedded couple on a honeymoon when they don't know I have been kidnapped by this handsome looking doctor who is Richie rich and also owns a private jet. At this point I don't doubt he could easily bring me to a vacant island and held me hostage and my breathe hitched when I thought about the actual possibility of it.

"Where the fuck are we?!", I demanded and he smirked looking down at me in amusement before answering.

"Any place in this world would be better than the city of love to get you know me? Besides its also your favourite city, am I wrong, hummingbird?".

I gaped at him in disbelief with my jaw open and I gasped covering my mouth with my palm.

SKILLED SMILE

"You brought me to fucking Paris?!!!!".

CHAPTER NINETEEN

RAFAEL'S POV

"Aren't you getting too much comfortable with cursing?", I ask her raising my right eyebrow and she scoffs folding her hands on her chest as I dropped her on the car seat. Scoffing as she waved her hand in between us and snapped, "What can I say, you bring worst out of me".

I smirked and said, "And you my hummingbird, brings best out of me".

I saw her clench her jaw as she rolled her eyes turning her head right side avoiding my gaze and tension filled between us again.

"When are we going back?", Isabella asked after sighing loudly gaining my attention back on her on our way to the penthouse I booked for this trip.

"We will be going back after celebrating new year here", I said not wanting to spoil her mood more than already I did.

"What the hell?! My friends will be back and will search for me! You can't keep...", I smirked as I cut her off.

"You don't want your friends to find about us, hummingbird?".

"Asshole, nope, there isn't any relationship between us, if there is it's kidnapper and victim, you ugly pathogen", she snapped and my smirk widened.

Placing my hand on my heart I faked hurt and said, "By the looks right now, I look victim and you my kidnapper".

"Ughhh, you crazy little piece...", she gasped in between her sentence when I pulled her off her seat and settled her on my lap with her thighs straddling mine and traced her hip curves as I spoke against her parted lips.

"There is nothing *little* related to me, hummingbird, don't embarrass yourself using wrong vocabulary", I whispered and she shivered on my lap making my cock twitch to life.

with my thumbs rubbing her inner thighs over her jeans I looked at her before revealing just enough for her to keep shut the whole trip.

"I told them that you are where you should be right now".

Gulping down she peered into my eyes with a frown marrying her face she scoffed, "Where? On my kidnapper's laps?".

Smacking her ass just little to shut her down I was able to bring a gaspy moan out of her to my amusement and her face turned red as she covered her mouth with her palms in embarrassment.

Smirking at her I answered, "Nope, with your boyfriend on a holiday".

She widened her eyes animatedly laughed throwing her head back and the space filled with her beautiful laughter.

"You... you know that they wouldn't trust anything about this if they don't hear from me?", she asked still laughing at me but my poker face made her doubt her words as her face suddenly married a frown and she inquired narrowing her eyes at me, "What did you do?, I know you did something".

"Uhm, I might or might not have done something that made them trust me but believe me, hummingbird, they are naming our ships, my personal favourite is rabella, that would suit our baby girl", I was cut off with a angry gasp from Isabella and I simply shrugged my shoulders smirking.

"Ughhh, what in this world is wrong with you! You cannot imagine having kids with me!", she exclaimed angrily and I bit my cheek telling I have did more than that but she is right. I never imagined having a child with Annabella but I didn't think a second for telling I want kids from Isabella?!

I guess that's the level of insane she turned me into. Isabella really fucked up my head making me insanely obsessed with her.

"Why? What's wrong with the idea, hummingbird? Because of you sitting comfortably on my dick, that's what I could only think about", I retorted and her eyes widened as he sprung into action by jumping off me and I chuckled enjoying her flustered face and her little innovative way of cursing me, "Psychodoc".

In few minutes we were passing through the street close to Eiffel tower and Isabella was admiring it with literally stars in her eyes. This immediately brought a smile on my face. Like a little kid, her joy was vibrating off her and I could literally feel it in my heart. I guess I made a good decision bringing her to Paris, if she is amazed by this now, she is going to freaking love it with what I have planned for her tonight and I can't wait to see that look in her eyes.

After checking into penthouse suite I hired I made sure someone have brought the clothes I ordered online on my way to Paris knowing Isabella wouldn't be any help by me forcing her out on a date.

As the shopping bags of expensive branded clothes I bought for her to wear them while we are in Paris are sitting on the bed, Isabella gawked at me with her jaw hanging down.

SKILLED SMILE

"Get ready hummingbird, we are leaving on our first date in an hour", saying that I exited the penthouse so that I could do final arrangements of the location and how I want ambiance to be.

Just to make sure everything is perfect for my hummingbird.

CHAPTER TWENTY

ISABELLA'S POV

Everything is beautiful, Paris is indeed city of love and people here are kind and welcoming. Though I didn't want to enjoy my time here but this city is sinfully beautiful just like Rafael.

My eyes widened and my hands flew to my mouth as I internally cursed myself for thinking about him like this.

"Ughh, you idiot, you stupid ass", I yelled throwing myself on bed and it bounced me making me yelp and laugh. Again... am not here to enjoy, yes I always wanted to come here but with my loved ones, with a guy who would knew me inside and out not with my freaking kidnapper who dragged me out of NewYork to Paris suddenly after ordering me to be his girlfriend.

And I shouldn't start about what he would have told my friends because that would make me more anxious than I have been and I don't want this stress to eat my energy out when I should be spending it in planning how to annoy Rafael and make him realize that am nothing special to be obsessed with so that he drop me right away at my home instead of thinking about caging me.

I jumped off from the bed excited as a brilliant idea rushed inside my head. Clapping my hands in excitement I went and took a quick shower and stormed out of en suite in lightening speed wearing a expensive pair of matching inner garments Rafael bought under the bathrobe.

Taking all the date night kind of dresses from the bags named brands like Gucci, Prada, Louis Vuitton, Dior and what not! Smirking I put them together on the floor and grab alcohol from the bar in the corner of the room and emptied few bottles on the clothes piled up and took the lighter from the same place and light it up smirking and there is no doubt people would think am a nut case if they look me right now.

SKILLED SMILE

Throwing the lit up lighter I saw the fire embracing the clothes and burn them and I sat back comfortably when the door burst open and I saw a freaked out rafael just in a towel wrapped around his torso and I smirked knowing the reason behind his fear very well that he heard the fire alarm go on.

His features eased when he found me sitting on bed and ran towards me engulfing me in a protective hug and behind him few staff rushed to set the fire off.

Examining me if am hurt he sighed in relief hugging me back and I froze in his arms looking how devastated he was. He thought I was hurt or dead? He was indeed really worried about me with the way he is holding me as if his life depends on me.

"Are you okay, baby? Fuck I was so scared!", he asked and I meekly nodded my head looking into his eyes trying to ignore the fact that am pressed against his naked and wet chest.

~

RAFAEL'S POV

"Yeah, I want the table to be decorated with more flowers, red and white roses precisely", I said to the florist on phone and heard a "Will be done", from him as I entered the penthouse. Hanging up the phone happy with the view and setup I smiled thinking how Isabella would react to it. I put my coat on the couch of the leaving room and made my way towards my bedroom and took a quick shower. Whistling a random tune I opened the closet to grab tonight's outfit then suddenly I heard

SKILLED SMILE

fire alarm ring and my body froze for a second then I threw the outfit on the bed and ran straight towards Isabella's room alerting staff pressing the emergency button on my way.

Thankfully the door of her room was open I saw her sitting on the bed and I sighed internally calming my racing heart which was almost blasting with the fear of losing her or seeing her hurt.

Ignoring the pile of burning clothes I rushed towards Isabella and hugged her tightly in my arms relieved that she is here, near me, in my arms and I won't let anything harm her. The staff members came almost behind me, prepared for many situations like this and put the fire off using the fire extinguisher and I examined her hands and legs if she accidentally hurt herself knowing that she did put that fire on. Thankfully I didn't find any injury on her and thanked God internally and when the fear eased in my body calming my racing heart my jaw clenched in anger.

Angry on the hotel and their staff, not on Isabella who put fire to the clothes I bought for her. "How the fuck you have this low safety measures?! Why weren't the sprinkles were on?!", I yelled at the staff and Isabella flinched in my hold at my harsh voice.

"We are sorry sir, there must be some defects and we will work on it, we are really sorry for this", one of the staff said and I glared at them tightening my hold on Isabella not hard enough to hurt her.

"You are sorry now?! What would you be if my girlfriend was hurt? If something happened to her?! You would tell a fucking sorry to my face?!", I seethed at them putting out the anger rumbling in my chest.

"Let your manager know am suing your hotel", I declared one last time and gestured them to leave the place immediately with my eyes and they did knowing talking to me about this matter won't help them.

"This was my fault you don't have to sue them", Isabella whispered exhaling on my chest and I groaned internally before looking at her.

Her face doesn't have the smirk she had before when I stepped in the room and she is now feeling guilty for what she did. As mad as I am on her right now, am also relieved that this didn't happen in other situation. The fire could have been a accident which we wouldn't have any idea about, I might have been out and no one here to save Isabella. The only thought of it sent shivers to my spine. Mentally making note to book another place for us to stay I looked at deer like doe eyes and whispered against her mouth.

"You could have hurt yourself".

"I... I don't have anything to wear on the date you are planning to take me", she whispered back showing very well that she is happy with the outcome of her plan.

I smirked enjoying her bratty side and pushed her wet locks behind her ear as I said, "Sweetheart, you didn't have to do that, if you wanted to make our date more special by wearing my shirt, you could have just asked".

As my words settled between us she clenched her jaw and pushed me away but I didn't move an inch and tightened my hold on her. Though it was amusing how she thought burning the clothes I bought for her could piss me off and she could have escaped the date but no, she is in delusion if she thinks she can escape from my cage, tonight she could have hurt herself and if I didn't warn she will repeat this.

Biting my cheek I twisted her hands behind not too hard that would bruise her, holding her jaw with my fingers I glared at her as I gritted out, "You thought this was funny, hummingbird? Huh?".

Her eyes glistened with tears as she tried to free herself from my hold. "Let me tell you what is funny – this", I said gesturing between us.

"How you think you could be free from my cage... is funny, thinking I will leave you if you throw some tantrums – is funny", I proclaimed looking straight into her glossy eyes which teared up more with my every word.

"Because you are mine and I embrace all of you, your perfects to your scars, your best and your worst, your tears to your smiles....you are all mine", I told and meant every fucking word I said.

Closing her eyes she let tears fall and I wiped them gently before pressing a kiss on her eyes and said, "Stop fighting, hummingbird, I might be caging you but am doing this to not loose you, too afraid that you will fly away from me as every best thing do".

With that I left her and walked out of the room towards my own. Closing the door behind me I punched the wall in anger and frustration. Pushing my wet hair behind I sighed drying them

SKILLED SMILE

with a towel and put on a blue jeans and white hoodie knowing very well that she won't be coming to any where I want to take her. But that doesn't mean I will let her go, specially not now – when her life is in danger.

Getting in my bed with a book knowing I won't be falling asleep with any pills or alcohol I open the book where I stopped reading last time. Wearing my reading glasses I read two to three pages and I heard a knock on the door.

Sighing to myself I put finger in between before closing the book and said, "Get in".

Isabella slowly opened the door revealing herself in a black oversized hoodie and blue faded jeans and smiled awkwardly before asking, "Is the date you begged for still up?".

I chuckled throwing my head back, I couldn't help. "I see a thief here", I commented eying my hoodie she was wearing.

Shrugging her shoulders she retorted, "Stealing from thief, isn't called stealing".

I raised my eyebrow amused, "Then what is it called Miss Isabella Miller?".

Scoffing as she rolled her eyes before threatening, "Doctor waldorf seems not interested in taking his bird on a date?".

CHAPTER TWENTY ONE

ISABELLA'S POV

I sat back on the bed too shocked with the words rafael said. I couldn't have believed or trust them if I haven't seen it in his eyes. He isn't lying and that made his every claim meaningful or

SKILLED SMILE

something I would consider an effort. No one has said such words to me and if I forget he kidnapped me, I would have been already head over heels for this man. Wiping my tears I smiled softly looking at the bag I packed. I didn't pack much clothes but I may have packed some hoodies I stole from rafael's wardrobe. In my defence, they are comfortable.

Wearing the most comfortable hoodie over a t shirt, I wore a body warmer under my jeans and blow dried my hair then applied strawberry flavoured lip balm and avoided makeup leaving my freckles uncovered.

If he wants to get me know him, I will and if I don't understand him..... Better he leave me or else the bird who's wings have been tied can bite and claw too.

Standing in front of his bedroom door I took a deep breath, it's now or never, I can go and talk to him and practically take him on the date or I could go back to my room and sleep tonight off. When I knocked the door ignoring pounding heart in my chest rafael's deep and hoarse voice called me in and my breathe hitched when I laid my eyes on him. He was wearing the most casual outfit and with the reading glasses on, with a book in his hand, he looked ethereal.

Not letting my hormones expose the effect he caused I cleared my throat and spoke daringly but I swear, I was sweating under my skin if it was possible.

~

Thankfully I didn't need to force him. wearing jackets over our causal outfits we sat in the front seats of the car without talking anything as rafael kept driving. The streets of Paris was ready to

SKILLED SMILE

welcome Santa Claus, the lights and Christmas trees and people carrying gifts it's clear that they all are excited for Christmas which is tomorrow and I will be lying if I said I wasn't jealous of everyone walking around visiting their families and spending another amazing Christmas of their lives with their loved ones.

I frowned, I didn't realize I was frowning until rafael's fingers eased the crease on my forehead. Giving me a small encouraging smile he showed me towards his side of the window which has a beautiful view of Eiffel tower.

Blinking with the lights it stood out in the darkness of the night. I smiled widely and enjoyed the view as we kept reaching close to it.

"Climb up", rafael said and I looked at him then back at the roof of the car where he gestured and smiled widely when the sunroof of the car opened.

"Oh my god!", I gasped as I stood on the seat of the car and felt the cold air hit my upper body. Opening my arms wide I laughed, giggled and wolf whistled enjoying the freedom one would love.

I was so into enjoying the moment that I didn't notice there weren't anyone near Eiffel tower and rafael drove the car right under the Eiffel Tower and I gasped in awe and my heart swelled with joy and my eyes twinkled with the lights blinking on the wonderful structure.

The car halted near the table which was covered with a picnic blanket and my cheeks literally hurt because of the wide smile painted on my face. Getting down from the car, I followed rafael when he held my hand and guided me towards the table and the heels of my boots dug in the layer of snow.

Whole place was decorated with my favourite red and white roses and white Chinese lathers and I almost teared up when he slid the chair for me.

Sitting on the comfortable cushion I smiled widely at rafael who's face reciprocated same joy and happiness as mine but I know his reasons are different than mine. I was happy because I was living my dream and he was happy because he made my dream come true.

This time a lone tear escaped my eyes and I wiped them discreetly as he ordered food for us. Again my favourite pizza, pasta and cheesecake along with coke and hot chocolate. When he served me a good amount of food I eyed his plate which had only salad which he usually eats at night claiming it's healthy and secret of his Greek god like body. Shaking my head in disagreement I shoved a spoonful of pasta in his mouth and his lips tugged up as he chewed on it.

"These are my favourite", I said and my voice breaking at the end and I cleared up covering it with a small cough.

Smiling widely he replied, "I know".

I admired how his blue eyes were shining and his smile alone could kill anyone. We enjoyed our late night meal laughing and giggling making silly comments as he told me about himself.

SKILLED SMILE

So my kidnapper was born in a middle class family and worked his ass off to be in the position where he is now, he made fortune out from nothing with his own hard work that now he could afford to make a public place like Eiffel tower to private on Christmas Eve. Owning many chains of hospitals all over America he also have special research centre where they invent medicines for the incurable diseases. The way he speaks amaze me, he hold maturity in his body language as well as in his words which I don't doubt – he could be crush of every second woman walking beside him.

His chiselled jaw was peppered with well trimmed beard just enough for one to imagine how it would feel poking on their neck when he hugs from behind. His electric blue eyes are deeper than the ocean, his smile could make you smile and his laughter would make your skin tingle. I found myself smiling at him unknowingly and gulped when he flexed his muscles pushing his jet black hair back.

"Thank you so much", I tell honestly looking into his eyes which were twinkling as if he have more to show and I smiled questioning him with my eyes.

As he clapped his hands twice a guy came out of nowhere and handed me a guitar and I gasped looking at rafael.

"Rafael!", I exclaimed when I understood what he was doing. He is fulfilling my Pinterest board goals. Trip to Paris during Christmas, picnic under Eiffel tower, singing on the Paris street at midnight…..

SKILLED SMILE

I don't even want to talk more about my other pins when he sat back on the hood of his car folding his hands on his chest with a eager look on his face I smiled shaking my head.

"What do you want me to sing?", I asked walking towards him and he thought for a second tapping on his chin cutely and I fought urge to aww and pinch his cheeks.

"How about the one you sang in the park before you met that Chinese kid?", he said and I gawked at him in shock.

"You were stalking me?!", I pointed my finger at him as I gasped narrowing my eyes.

Raising his hands in surrender he shrugged his shoulders and a cheeky smirk made it's way on his handsome face that definitely bought him a point.

Ughh, bella! Get yourself together!

Scolding myself internally I sighed sitting on the bench near the lake and the ambiance alone gave me chills beside the thick snow under my boots. Taking a deep breathe, I smiled.

Then started singing the song I wrote.

I have few scars no one has ever seen

I will let you trace them with your fingertips

The smiles I wear on my lips is fake

Because I believe no one cares

Darling, Will you help me change my view?

SKILLED SMILE

By pulling me out from the darkness of my room?

Will you wipe those invisible tears on my cheeks?

Bringing a real smile on my lips

Am tired being strong

Will you be that someone I could lean on

My tears are invisible but my eyes are not nil

I have my love stored in them for you....

I couldn't sing further, I felt vulnerable, the lyrics I wrote were from the depth of my heart and I feel it as no one would. Indeed listeners would feel the lyrics but only writers could feel the pain behind those lyrics and to master the art of understanding it, it takes listeners to go through the same pain. Closing my eyes tightly, fighting the tears threatening to fall I bit my lip to stop it from quivering as I avoided meeting rafael's gaze whole time.

Then I heard his voice, melodic, deep, painful, passionate as he gently took away the guitar from me. Then I snapped my eyes open to look at him with my glossy ones, his blue eyes were dull and I have no idea about the reason which made joy from his eye colour fade. He planned this date to get me know him but I learnt what he told not what his eyes spoke and suddenly I had an urge to read them, drown it them finding answers to the questions I didn't ask and a lone tear escaped my eyes when he sang, matching my tune even without the music... he touched my soul as I never thought one would. Bringing me on my feet he placed his hand on my waist and intertwined his other hand with my cold ones. Closing my eyes I heard the way he sang and the lyrics bore in my heart.

Because you are my love…

You are the reason to love…

I am obsessed with being in love with you…

That I would die when you leave me too…

Darling,

I have few scars I never knew…

Am not afraid to show them to you

because I know, you will trace them with your love…

We are two halves of a rainbow

Lean on me and I will hold

Fighting the storms of our lives

We will grow old…

CHAPTER TWENTY TWO

RAFAEL'S POV

SKILLED SMILE

She cried, big fat tears tainted her face, her nose and cheeks turned redder than before when she bit her lip and sobbed. I held her in my arms afraid she would break any second and I was read to fix her broken pieces together. When she opened her eyes she smiled, true and honest smile one could give. Just as a child smiles at its mother, her lips widened as her eyes teared up and then she cradled my face in her tiny palms and I understood what she wants, I want it too. Not because it's one of her pin in Pinterest board but to seal the feelings which bloomed between us. It's true as fuck that *I am not just obsessed with her, am fucking obsessed with loving her.*

She is like my broken piece of heart, it fits perfectly in the hole I have and I want to cage her there eternally. Bending down a little I pulled her up in my arms with my both hands on her waist and she leaned her forehead on mine and said, "I am not sorry for this".

Honestly she didn't need to tell that because I already knew, we won't regret this, if we do – we would regret not listening to our hearts.

"Neither do I, nor for the first one, this or all others I will share with you in future till my last breath", as soon as I said those words I smashed my lips on hers. Slowly, gently, passionately I moved them against hers and she mirrored me. Kissing me back she bit my lip and I smirked in between the kiss squeezing her waist and she moaned.

Fuck!

Deepening the kiss I grabbed her nape still keeping one hand on her waist, I pulled her close to me and traced her lower lip with my tongue asking her to open her mouth and she did. Thrusting my tongue inside her mouth, I kissed her deeply exploring every inch of her mouth. Her sweetness blasted on my taste buds and I grew harder in my pants at the thought of devouring her completely leaving no inch of her body un kissed.

"Uhmm", she moaned breathless in my arms when I sucked on her tongue and she did same with mine following my lead and I saw fucking stars. Pouring our unsaid words into each other without speaking we kissed as our life depends on it and slowly broke the kiss keeping our foreheads attached as we caught our breathe.

Still with her closed eyes she smiled shyly opening her doe eyes she blinked looking at me as if I was a rainbow and I smiled before I said, "It's snowing, rockstar, am sorry I couldn't show you rainbow on this lake right now".

She chuckled knowing that was her another pin and her voice swayed me in delight when she said, "I saw it, you are my rainbow, doctor rafael".

ISABELLA'S POV

Try asking a orphan when they felt connected with a person when they don't know what it is to be connected to someone – by blood, by heart, by soul… not just physically but mentally – not mentally, *emotionally!*

Neither someone have did something like this for me before nor said anything that healed my soul. On the right time, in the wrong way, I found a right person. I will be damned if I let him go but would he let me go?

I don't want to think about it after spending a beautiful night of my life… which I beg to last a little bit longer. Glancing at rafael now and then I found his eyes on the road, not a blink of sleep his eyes reflect as if he is a robot. I yawn, tiredly.

"Aren't you sleepy?", I ask breaking the silence which gained his attention.

"You can sleep, hummingbird, traffic is tight as it's Christmas", he said and I blinked my heavy eyes.

I don't want to sleep but I was tired and wondered if this doctor have any special medicine to not fall asleep. Giggling to myself internally I felt my eyes slowly shut looking at rafael.

~

Waking up I stretched my body tiredly and squirted my eyes. Scanning my surroundings. I frowned finding myself in different place than we were before, yawning I saw time and it was almost four a.m. and I frowned. I slept for two hours! There is no doubt rafael tucked me in my bed when I was sleeping as a horse.

Is he asleep? I shook my head before getting out of bed and walked out of my room and saw rafael working on the MacBook. Looking around once again I saw this place was more European style than the modern one where we stayed before.

"You didn't go to bed?", I asked as I saw him rubbing his eyes tiredly staring at the screen. Sighing he diverted his eyes off the screen and looked at me before shrugging his shoulders.

"I am not sleepy", he said and his voice spoke something else. Scowling I walked towards him and he straightened himself on the couch and made some space for me to sit.

Pressing my palm on his forehead I examined earning a chuckle from him.

"You aren't sick doc!", I told smirking and sat beside him with a sigh.

"Why did you wake up?", he asked diverting the subject and I rubbed my hands together before replying.

"I like to cuddle my teddy bear when I sleep, I get restless when am alone for a long time", I tell gulping down the uneasiness of opening up to someone.

His hand immediately landed on my thigh and I turned to look into his eyes before I spoke.

"We all have demons, some doesn't let sleep, some makes you want to sleep for forever, Doctor Waldorf", I said pressing my lips together and his face tensed but he asked, "What are yours, hummingbird?".

I exhaled heavily fighting the multiple voices in my head before I decided to speak about them for the first time.

"I don't remember much about my childhood….. Actually I don't even remember anything, not even how my parents look", I said and his face was emotion less, not giving away anything what he was thinking and that somewhat encouraged to speak me because I don't like people pity me.

SKILLED SMILE

"I remember this white room, which has a chair and I... I... I couldn't breathe, one door, chocolates wrappers in my hand and someone... someone who's name is Eden", I said closing my eyes to point out one thing I know about that person or at least if he was real.

"What's funny is..... I don't even know if these are my nightmares or my reality and honestly I can't digest the fact if it's real, I badly want that to be nightmares", I admitted opening my eyes to look into his azure eyes.

"You should accept them, because the hardest part was over, suffering – is the hardest part, hummingbird", he said and I chuckled humourlessly.

"Doctor Waldorf, if that was real, you would have been sleeping right now", I said and his jaw clenched and then unclenched.

"Suffering is weakest part, doctor Waldorf, accepting – is the hardest part", I said and he scowled shaking his head.

"My demons are different than your, I remember everything, I embraced them but I couldn't find peace because I know, I didn't suffer – others did – because of me", he said gulping and his Adams apple bobbed as his veins turned visible on his neck and forehead.

"I was the reason nearly forty members hoping to live.......died", he revealed and I gasped in disbelief earning a humourless chuckle from him.

CHAPTER TWENTY THREE

RAFAEL'S POV

"Don't look at me like that, you should be looking at me as if am a murderer, a killer", I gritted out looking into her eyes which were showing disbelief, shock.

Clearing her throat she folded her legs on couch turning towards me as if kids sit around granny's chair when she is going to read them a story book. "Why would I judge you with little information you gave me? I would like to know more besides am not someone who judge others", she said pressing her plump lips together and fought the urge to trace them with my thumb.

Looking between her lips then her eyes which were waiting for answers I decided to tell her just as much as she needed to know.

"When I was a kid, I saw my mother fight cancer", I said keeping my voice constrained.

Her brows furrowed in sympathy and she reached for my hand and I let her hold it. Tracing circles between my thumb and index finger she gazed at me giving me a assuring smile which made me smile back at her.

Exhaling heavily I spoke, "She suddenly decided to stop fighting because she was too tired and eventually I was left alone, my father was never in the picture, never saw him", I said remembering how my mother said he didn't wanted her nor me.

What is worse? Growing up knowing our parents were dead or knowing they threw you out of their life because they never wanted you? In either way they are dead but honestly, the one who lives around you – lives in your memories, when they die

SKILLED SMILE

you carry their smiles but the parent who never wanted you – you carry their burden, disappointment and the way they made you feel you aren't important in their lives which eventually puts you in pressure to be important to someone, no matter how much they force you to change, you cross your own breaking point to be just important to them. I did – everything I could but I was never enough for Annabella, if I was, she wouldn't have done what she did. I didn't realize I was squeezing Isabella's hand tightly as I was in my train of thoughts until she hissed in pain.

Immediately I left her hand then examined if I hurt her too much. "I'm so sorry, I was… just… fuck! am sorry".

"It's okay, rafael, am fine", she said assuring me showing her hand and I sighed in relief.

"I understand it might be hard for you tell what and how it happened, I will wait if you need time, it's not like am actually a hummingbird who would fly away from the window", she joked trying to ease the tension radiating through me.

Shaking my head as no I nodded towards the bar. "I just need a drink, want to have some?", I ask her and she smiled shyly before shaking her head as no.

"I don't drink much, thank you", she denied politely and I smiled pouring myself a glass of Bourbon. Sitting on the high chair I turned around to look at her as I spoke.

"After my mother's death because of cancer I wanted to save people so that their loved ones don't go through the same pain as mine, I wanted to save people's lives, So studying hard, I invented a vaccine, which would not only treat cancer patients of any stage but also would avoid the disease permanently", I said and her eyes beamed with pride.

Gulping the sweet and oak flavoured Bourbon I let the taste linger on my tongue before pouring another glass. "Someone – I trusted stole the batch which was going to be given to thirty seven cancer patients who were hopeful that they were going to live but......", I said taking a deep breathe and clenched the glass hard in my hand unable to describe how painful death they went through. How could I tell that they felt their skin burn and flesh shed off their bones as their blood turned acidic in their body, experiencing burning every single nerve and tissue they died begging for death.

Suddenly I felt her tiny figure trying to hug me with her arms around my shoulders and struggling to do so as I was on a high chair. Wanting to feel her, feel some sort of assurance I fell on my knees and she hugged me as I broke down. I wouldn't wanted anyone to see me in this state, in my weakest state as I cried in arms of someone who is more broken than me but I accepted.

I accepted it wasn't my fault, trusting someone is not ones fault because they did what they were asked of. I trusted Annabella because she made me believe her, she asked me to believe her and it's her fault that people died. It's her fault not mine and I hugged Isabella tightly as I cried in her arms. Last time I cried was holding my mother and the comfort I found in her was never found in someone else but in Isabella..... I feel sheltered.

"It's okay.....", she cooed running her hands in my hair and I exhaled heavily.

"You are not killer or murderer rafael, you didn't kill them, you are innocent… in fact you are strong enough to fight with god, he is the only one who holds the power of life and death and *you doctors fight with him and win*", she said with a shaky breathe.

"If you lose someday you just have to understand, you aren't god, you know taste of failure you will crave for success, everything will be fine one day", she assured and I found myself smiling.

Breaking the hug I looked up to her and she smiled and then I noticed she was crying too. Wiping her own tears she wiped mine and I closed my eyes feeling her touch on my skin. Then I told, "Eden, the boy you keep dreaming about… is real".

Her fingers halted hearing the truth I said. Looking into her eyes this time I said, "We both were in the same orphanage, I am Eden, rockstar and am sorry".

CHAPTER TWENTY FOUR

ISABELLA'S POV

Three months since rafael said he was Eden and eventually that said my nightmares were real. After celebrating new year in Paris we returned back to NewYork and this time he decided to cage me in a different mansion close to his workplace. I didn't fight him after that night.

~Three months ago~

"You are my girlfriend, hummingbird, you will stay with me", he declared buttoning up his shirt. I clenched my jaw in anger and strolled towards him punching him on his shoulder.

"Just because I kissed you twice that doesn't mean I am your girlfriend you filthy airborne disease!", I gritted out and he threw his head back and laughed till his eyes glistened and I bit my cheek to not comment –how handsome he looks when he laugh.

"If you fight like this… I will never complain about you fighting", he said and I rolled my eyes.

"Doctor Waldorf… don't ruin your 'workaholic-handsome bachelor' image by talking about our ship names you dream about naming our kids and now thinking about how you have any chance fighting me in the future", I retorted folding my hands on chest.

He smirked cockily before cornering me in his walk in closet, staling me as a predator and I gulped taking each step away from

SKILLED SMILE

him just to be struck in between him and the mirror. My heart beat rose, thundering in my chest and to make sane distance between our bodies I put my hands on his chest and he smirked again.

"Rockstar...", he whispered in my ear and goose bumps peppered on my skin and my breathe hastened.

"For you... I won't think twice about ruining my workaholic image and settle down as a family man because you are the only one in whom I find peace", he revealed and I clenched his shirt in my palms and tried to push him away.

"It's not about you! what about me? I have my friends and my own life, doctor waldorf.... You can't keep me locked in as if am some animal to entertain you", I snapped and his face tensed up in distaste of words I used.

"Look, Lisa and I share a place, we both can't afford the whole place alone and she took me in when I was in need, I sing with them on streets because we are saving the money to debut as a band one day when we work our asses off doing odd jobs so that we have food, roof and clothes! I can't leave my friends just because you are obsessed with me!!!", I said exhaling heavily.

"Please try to understand, Eden, because of you I can't change my life, that's not fair...... I promised to understand you, am trying, am here...", I said truthfully and a lone tear escaped my eyes.

"Shhh, I hate seeing tears in your eyes", he said wiping my tears lovingly and I closed my eyes as I said, "Then stop making me cry".

"You are my girlfriend, hummingbird, you are not safe singing on the streets, the word of our dating didn't spread in media yet... I don't want to take chance, it's dangerous", he said and I sighed too tired to talk back now.

"I will take care of everything, in fact I wanted to ask – why you guys haven't started posting your music on YouTube?", he asked and I gawked at him with my furrowed eyebrows.

"What?!", I asked in disbelief and he smiled before pressing his lips on my forehead and said, "Now be a good girl for me until I come back".

~Now~

"Good girl, hummingbird, rockstar, sweetheart.....", Lisa sighed with a smirk on her face and dropped herself on the couch.

"Lisa...", I warned her to not speak anything and she ignored my warning as she spoke to Nick who was fixing camera in the garden wanting to shoot our first YouTube video outdoor since the weather in NewYork by the end of march is all warm and we could practically feel spring approaching as the trees wrapped themselves with new green leaves.

"Nick, tell me something, why the fuck she isn't in love with the doctor A.O.W.Y who kidnapped her just to take her to her dream vacation in his private jet, practically never let her do anything with all the maids in honour to do the house chores, keeps her in a palace like mansion which is fucking 10,000 square feet! Buys her everything she doesn't ask to everything she needs and encouraged to start up a YouTube channel, which I don't think any other kidnapper would have done", she said in awe then looked back to me with guilty expression on her face when Nick added, "Baby you are forgetting that they both have kissed twice on lips and sleep in the same bed, she sings for him and he let her cuddle him".

I clenched my jaw as I snapped my fingers ready to throw some fist at my so called best friend. "Lisa! You are dead— dead", I announced as I jumped to catch her but she ran screaming for help.

"Please, am sorry, I didn't wanted to tell but you know I couldn't keep it as a secret from nick!", she screamed running away with a throttle of laughter behind her.

"You backstabber! What else did you tell him?!", I gritted out running behind her to catch her as fast as I could.

"Uhmm, might be that you have felt his morning wood as you sleep in the same bed and you are not as innocent as you used to be?", she yelled as she increased her speed and I felt my face turn red in embarrassment and saw around if someone might have heard us but thankfully I found none around.

"Lisa! Am going to kill you!", I snapped and started running again and this time I decided to take short cut since I wasn't able to match her speed.

Running into the pool area I decided to surprise her by standing right in front of her. Snickering evilly I thought the ways I would punch her when I get my hands on her but my voice died in my throat when I ran into a wall – at least that's what I thought and I hissed and stumbled looking at rafael with wide eyes as I was falling back into the pool. Rafael immediately wrapped his arm around my waist and fell along with me instead of stopping our fall.

Falling into the warm water with a splash as my scream echoed in the pool area I have no doubt that we gathered audience.

"Ugh! You were supposed to save me! not fall along with me!", I scolded him swimming on the top of the water as I wiped water off my face.

My organza dress decided to keep floating in the warm water enjoying it's own time as I usually wash it in cold water. At this rate my panties should be blessing the floor of the pool with parental advisory content and I sighed when rafael held me so that I got the chance to keep my dress down.

But then I realized something which made my skin turn red and my eyes widened as I asked.

"Please don't tell me you were skinny dipping".

CHAPTER TWENTY FIVE

RAFAEL'S POV

I smirked. I couldn't help. "If you don't want to hear what you already figured out then... no, hummingbird, I wasn't skinny dipping, I just got out of the swimming pool after skinny dipping but you decided to slam into me", I said shrugging my shoulders tightening my hold on her.

"You are naked, like naked – naked?", she asked with tiny hope of having me covered in a piece of cloth but I was as naked as the day I was born.

I shook my head and my lips twitched when she jumped away from me but I kept her pressed against my body and the only fabric left between us wasn't enough to not let me feel her every curve.

My cock grew harder when she struggled in my arms and I groaned unable to succumb the natural cause which she makes happen almost every minute she looks at me.

"Are you okay? We heard you scream", said Lisa and I groaned mentally. Following her, nick walked and his eyes widened as well as lisa's when they saw the state Isabella and I was.

"Oh my fucking goodness! Did you scream without s?", Lisa asked and Isabella gasped then shook her head vigorously making animated moves as no and I smirked.

"No! fuck no! I didn't!", she tried to convenience them and they smirked not believing.

"Upset you didn't *scream without s*, hummingbird, I can make you if you want", I whispered in her ear making sure this stays between us two.

Her eyes widened and she tried to push me off her but I held her tightly smiling at her mischievously.

"You want them to see me naked?", I asked her whispering and she scoffed rolling her eyes and snapped, "It's not my problem, you should have thought before going hakuna matata when we have guests in our home".

I smiled, genuinely. Isabella addressing this place as our home... made this place special for me. Not trying to hide how satisfied that answer made me I retorted.

"If you let them see me like this... there is no way they will think you are speaking truth".

Isabella opened her mouth to speak something but shut immediately understanding it's her win — win if she covers me up. She wouldn't have to go through the embarrassing conversation Lisa will force out of her.

"If you would have saved me, instead of falling with me, we wouldn't have to face this situation", Isabella gritted out and lisa and nick cleared their throats reminding us their unforgettable presence.

"Hummingbird, if I couldn't save you... I will fall with you", I said truthfully and she gazed in my eyes with her softened ones.

She didn't have to search for truth because I know she can see it clearly.

SKILLED SMILE

"I'm sorry, I was late, what you all are doing……", Bruce asked and his face twisted when he saw Isabella and me. Gulping down he smiled at Lisa and nick politely before winking at Isabella and I clenched my jaw.

Ignoring my presence he commented, "Remember when we used to go swimming? You used to look damn hot in your white bikini… how about we *friends* go again someday?"

Too oblivious to his intentions Lisa and nick smiled in agreement nodding their heads and my hummingbird awkwardly smiled uncomfortable about the way he complimented her. *My Good girl.*

I smirked, he told himself what he is – a friend, nothing more and I wrapped my arms around Isabella nuzzling my face in her neck and looked straight into Bruce's eyes as I said.

"If you all *friends* wait outside for us, we will come out of this pool ASAP, or at least we will try", I said smirking as I pressed my lips on Isabella's neck and she giggled. She is ticklish in between her neck and shoulder but no one needed to know that.

"Oh my god, come on let's give doctor A.O.W.Y some quality time with his hummingbird", Lisa said too excited and this is the only time I liked it. Bruce clenched his jaw and his hands turned into fists as he gave me one last sour look slowly walking behind lisa and nick and I smirked in victory.

Isabella is mine, fucking mine. The sooner he understand the better it is for him.

"Why the fuck you did that?!", Isabella snapped as fast as she found us alone.

"Did what? Kissed *my girlfriend*?", I asked raising my eyebrows innocently and she rolled her eyes.

"Dochole", she cursed under her breathe which is her another innovative profanity and I smiled.

"By the way, what does doctor A.O.W.Y means?", I asked as she pushed me off her and got out of the swimming pool.

"Doctor am obsessed with you", she yelled walking towards the towel rack and I smirked as I yelled back.

"I'm obsessed with you too, hummingbird".

"Of course", she scoffed shaking her head and I chuckled enjoying pissing her off.

But little did she know that am just obsessed with her am obsessed with loving her.

ISABELLA'S POV

"Perfect, I will upload it tonight as soon as possible", Lisa said after we recorded our first video. It's almost evening and rafael arranged lunch for all of us and Lisa couldn't stop gushing how perfect couple rafael and I look.

Honestly that made me giddy but I wouldn't admit it to her.

"Are you sure, internet doesn't work well in your apartment", Bruce asked and Lisa smiled widely before answering.

SKILLED SMILE

"Well, after Doctor Waldorf bought whole building, everything works perfect in every apartment".

Nick smiled pressing a kiss on lisa's lips and said, "As bella staying here we are having a great time fucking".

I cringed as well as Bruce but his face reflected that uneasiness I never saw before. "You mean fucking great time, don't talk without censor someone could have heard you and died of witnessing hyper carnal knowledge", I scoff and Lisa smirked.

"Another disease doctor taught you, hummingbird?", she commented and I saw Bruce clench his jaw as he jumped in between changing the topic thankfully.

"Have you finished writing that song? If you do, I will be the first one to hear it right?", he asked hopefully and I smiled at him widely.

"Of course, you will be the first one, bruce, after all you are my long time friend", I said and he winced making me frown.

"Are you okay?", I asked holding his arm and he looked where my hand is then back to my face before he nodded his head with a smile.

As he was about to hug me, rafael walked out of nowhere and pulled me against himself and I bit my cheek stopping myself from saying something rude.

"Where did you put my black hoodie, sweetheart?", he asked faking confusion.

"I don't know!", I said through my gritted teeth with a tight smile on my face.

"But last night you were the one wearing it", he revealed and my face paled in realization.

"Oh! That one, I removed it when I was in library, I might have forgot to take it from there", I said feeling sorry that I have used almost every hoodie from his wardrobe and usually forget them as I place them somewhere else when I feel too warm.

"It's okay, I will ask maid to get it", he said and I shook my head.

"They are almost leaving, sending them off I will come find it myself, Anastasia worked hard whole day", I said earning a smile from him.

"Okay", he said pressing his lips on my forehead and I blushing realizing how awkward our conversation would have been to my friends.

"I don't want you all to visit us tomorrow, I am taking my girlfriend on a date", he said and nick smiled genuinely and lisa winked at me.

"Forced girlfriend", bruce snapped and I frowned shaking my head as no so that I could stop rafael from losing his calm.

"Eden, please", I pleaded when he stormed towards bruce and he halted his steps immediately. "Please get inside, I will come back to you after sending them off", I whispered and he gave one long distasteful look to bruce before storming inside the mansion with his hands shoved in his trousers pockets.

I sighed then frowned at bruce, "He didn't hurt me, you don't have to get on his bad side for me", I said gaining a judgemental scowl from bruce. Folding his hands on his chest he scoffed glancing at Lisa and Nick. "And you guys say she doesn't love him, she obviously fell for all these!", he said and my eyes widened.

"What did you tell?!", I gritted looking at my friend in disbelief. How can my own friend think I fell in love with someone because they are rich?! "You think I will fall someone for these?", I asked ending the sentence with a humourless laugh.

"That's very low of you thinking about your best friend, bruce, you all can leave now", I said. Lisa and Nick nodded their heads in understanding and bruce retorted, "Then why don't you file a compliant against him?".

"I am dealing this as simple as any sane person would, bruce, he asked me to stay with him, so that I get to know him, if I couldn't...... I will leave him", I said honestly.

"Will he? Will he let you go?!", he asked as I turned around and walked towards the mansion. My steps halted and I took a deep breathe as I told, "At this rate I am afraid that I couldn't live if he let me go".

CHAPTER TWENTY SIX

RAFAEL'S POV

"Isabella...", I called her from behind and she suddenly jumped then sighed seeing me.

"Don't ever scare me like that!", she groaned and I smiled how cute she looks in her messy hair bun and night suit – *my hoodie* and random shorts.

"What are you doing at this time? Aren't you sleepy?", I asked walking towards her and sat beside the couch and she folded her legs comfortably sitting back and keeping her pen and book on her laps. Rubbing her tired eyes she answered, "I was writing lyrics for one of my songs which I started long time ago".

"I have no motivation to write this... it's struck awfully", she said groaning, clenching the pen in her hand. I frowned biting my lip as I thought any way I could help.

"What is this song about?", I asked and she pouted trying to find a perfect word and tapped pen on her plump lips. "Soulmate? Love? Better half?", she told shrugging her shoulders.

"Something like that... someone who saves you from your nightmares and keep you safe", she said looking into my eyes. I smiled, "Get your ass up, we are going out", I said and she whined.

"Not now, it's damn four a.m.!", she reasoned and I smiled cheekily. "Hurry up", I said dragging her along me holding the hood of my hoodie she is wearing.

SKILLED SMILE

"Oww, don't treat me as I am a cat!", she said and I chuckled. "Fine, you aren't a cat, you are *my kitten*", I said and she groaned kicking me on my calf playfully.

"Stop with those pet names, fucker, or else am going to strangle you with fucking cord of my mic one day", she threatened and I rolled my eyes.

"You wish, you want, you need are different feelings sweetheart... right now I want you to succumb your wish, forget what you want and need you to follow me", I said strictly not listening to her complaints telling how she isn't properly dressed. She is – if she is in my clothes, she is properly dressed.

~

"Did we reach?", she sang and I groaned internally.

"Did we reach?", she sang again and I wonder how the fuck she have this patience to annoy my ass asking same question for thousands of times. "Did we reach?", she screamed in my ear and I immediately pressed the breaks stopping the car in the corner.

The next moment I pulled her on me and she gasped. Her eyes widened as I held nape of her neck, pulling her close to me as our lips almost touched.

"I'm taking you to get you inspired to write love song, if you be a brat I swear to fucking god, Isabella..... You will be writing about the deeds done in bed by people in love", I warned circling my thumb on her sweet spot and she whimpered.

SKILLED SMILE

"You like that?", I asked and she mewled and her eyes widened at involuntary sound she released and she covered her mouth in embarrassment. Her neck and cheeks turned red as I smirked answering for her. "You love that".

My cock twitched in my pants and all I want to do is pound into her drawing out more sinful sounds she never imagined she could spill.

I groaned internally, throwing my head back and bit my cheek trying to kill unholy thoughts which felt so tempting to eschew.

Peering into her eyes, I whispered. "Don't look at me like that".

"Like what?", she asked taking her palm off her mouth and placing it on my chest and I groaned.

"Like you want my face between your legs", I said and she sucked in air and I saw how her chest rose and fell breaking my every level of sanity I was trying to keep around her.

ISABELLA'S POV

"I... I am not looking at you like that!", I squeaked and cursed myself internally for telling it in that tone. His blue eyes dilated leaving only a thin electric blue ring around the black core of his ethereal eyes and I awed internally how beautiful he looks like this.

His jet black hair was messed up as he kept running his hair in them when I annoyed the hell out of him on our way and right now if this is how I get to see him when I be a brat, I want to be a brat forever.

SKILLED SMILE

"Do you know what I like most about you, that you made me fucking obsessed?", he asked and I nodded my head getting lost in his eyes as his large palms rested on hips and I held my breathe.

"You are thoughtful, caring, loving and kind", he said and I exhaled shakily.

"Aren't those all same thing?", I asked and he smiled shaking his head. "No, rockstar, those four words could be synonyms to each other but they have different meaning", he said and I frowned.

Easing my tensed brow with his thumb he said, "You are thoughtful – when you put my need to be around you over the advice bruce gave to file complaint against me".

"You are kind – when you think about how hard Anastasia works and offer your help", he said pushing my curls back and I gapped at him.

"You are loving – when you spoke to the kid who approached you in the park", he told tracing his thumb on my freckles and I bit my lip.

"You are caring – when you didn't left your friends on their own when I promised you fucking world", he added and freed my lower lip from my teeth.

"These are all different and so you are, different person not like someone I associated in my whole life and I want to keep you with me, forever because I know you are the rarest diamond which this insane fucker found", he said and I closed my eyes when he moved his lips closer to me as they almost touched.

SKILLED SMILE

"Eden", I moaned and he brushed his nose with mine as he spoke against my lips. "Open your eyes rockstar", I compiled as he said.

Opening my eyes I saw into his blue eyes and with one look he gestured me to raise my head and when I did, I gasped. The sports car top was opened giving the best view of the sky I have ever seen in my life.

"Oh my god", I breathed out looking at the bright orange sky which was clear and rafael smiled at me as tears threatened to fall from my eyes.

"Explore the place hummingbird, hope it motivates you to write something good", he said and I looked into his eyes before asking, "Isn't your hummingbird supposed to be in your cage, Doctor Waldorf?".

He smiled, pressing his lips on my cheek he took me by surprise as he said, "For your safety I can keep you in my cage and for your freedom – I can break every fucking cage of the world".

I smiled and returned the gesture of sweet little kiss by pecking him on his cheek which made me feel thousands of butterflies in my stomach as my lips tingled. Smiling widely I got off the car and ran on the beach, taking off my footwear I ran barefoot in the cold sand. Ocean sang as it's waves carried the tune to my ears. The sun begun to rise higher with time and flocks of birds went to welcome it's presence encouragingly humming for another challenging yet beautiful day. I smiled widely spreading my hands wide and embraced the fresh air which is rare to experience in the New York city as I ran as a free spirit in the arms of nature.

SKILLED SMILE

My nightmares felt slipping off my head which kept me awake at nights and I kept it to myself to not stress rafael out. I started remembering few things, few faces I have never seen before but what was terrifying that she has different hair – blonde, straight hair precisely and grey eyes. I thought I was seeing my own reflection but no, I wasn't, my hair was still fiery orangish red.

I winced, those words…. *"Take Anna to the testing ground, keep this redhead here until my next order and make sure you keep her ready for tests"*.

Those words were said by the same voice, *"She is a failed project, a failure"*.

I didn't know I was on my knees facing ocean until rafael put his hand on my shoulder bringing me out of my train of thoughts.

"Eden", I gasped.

Frowning he sat beside me on the sand as we faced each other. "What's wrong, rockstar?", he asked. His voice dripping with worry and I sighed shaking my head.

"Are you having those nightmares again?", he asked and I chuckled looking at the sky.

"I don't know, Eden, at this point… I don't know what are nightmares and what is real", I said and he held my hand in his own and pressed a kiss on the back of my hand.

"Nightmares had a door between us rockstar, this……", he said gesturing to our intertwined hands and said. "Is real, we are together and whatever is scaring you….. Should go through me to reach you".

I teared up. I couldn't stop them at this moment, when I felt most vulnerable yet strong because Eden was with me, he was always was with me in my soul, in my head and in my dreams but now, he is real and I accepted the truth which I was afraid to realize. I indeed fell for my kidnaper, who stole my heart a very long time ago.

I smiled as he wiped my tears, "Go to hospital, Eden", I said and he agasted at my words but my next words made him kill his fear which haunted him – stopping him from treating people in need.

"Because you need to heal too and it will be only possible when you treat others, Doctor Waldorf".

CHAPTER TWENTY SEVEN

RAFAEL'S POV

"Patient in room number 204 should be strictly put on liquid diet and clear my daily examining schedule for the surgery we should carry tomorrow", I ordered and my PA smiled nodding his head, too happy I have taken in charge.

"I want file of patient's medical history to the type of medications he have taken around forty eight hours before surgery and keep me updated with patient's current situation so that if there is any emergency I don't want anyone delay the procedure", I ordered and he said, "Got it doctor".

After he left I sighed taking off my gloves and washed my hands twice with hand wash and the door of my office opened. Coming out of the washroom I saw Isabella removing her face mask and glasses which she is forced to wear because the popularity their channel grew.

"I think I should fire the bodyguards I hired for you, they didn't updated me that you are going to visit me", I said taking off my lab coat and she rolled her eyes.

"It's been a week I asked you to go back hospital and you never came back home before three a.m.", she complained slamming her hands on the office table and I smirked.

"Missing me, Rockstar?", I asked and she frowned eying the files on the table.

"Those are the files of the patients who are undergoing surgery this month", I said and her eyes softened as she looked at me.

"You might be stressed and tired", she said lifting a file and read it's name as we put name of the surgery and patient's code on the file and patient's name and details inside of the file for privacy.

"What is Posterior fossa decompression?", she asked and I put the file back in the place before answering her.

"It's a condition where we cut some part precisely back of the skull to decrease the pressure on the brain", I said and she grinned.

"Doctor Waldorf gets ten out of ten! Give a big round of applauds!", she hooted and I chuckled shaking my head.

"What do you want?", I asked clearly getting that she came here trying to convince me for something.

"Uhm, I mean... I came to meet you", she said scratching her forehead awkwardly and I narrowed my eyes on her.

"Okay! Fine! Don't look at me like that! I came here to ask if you could let me go to the spring carnival with my friends? Please...", she pleaded giving me her fucking puppy eyes and I sighed.

"Is this lisa's idea?", I asked and she nodded her head vigorously. "Then am coming too, I can't let you go with that crazy woman who may hang you off the ferries wheel for entertainment", I said and she glared at me folding her hands on her chest.

"I can take care of myself, doctor op, I don't want you tagging me behind everywhere I go! However your bodyguards won't let me breathe without asking your permission", she huffed and I kept my poker face.

"Either you are going with doctor over protective or you aren't going at all", I said using her the new nickname she gave me. she groaned stomping her leg glaring me as if she wants to choke me with the stethoscope hanging on my neck.

My stubborn Brat!

"Fine! Bring your ass home early so that we can leave at sharp four today evening", she ordered sassily before putting on her mask and glasses and walked out of the office shutting the door behind her loudly with a thud.

"Your girlfriend?", my PA asked and I smiled shaking my head and sat on my chair before answering, *"My world"*.

~

"Doctor Waldorf, you need to see this!", one of my research member stormed into my office and I scowled at him. Did he forgot basic knowledge of how to knock before entering his boss's cabin?!

"Miss Isabella's blood report...", he said gasping for air and I stood on my legs immediately.

"What's wrong?", I asked and my heart trembled in fear and my legs automatically stormed towards the research lab we have in the top floor of this building which is just above my office.

"I'm so sorry but it was urgent", he said and his words turned muffled in my ears. I couldn't see anything past something is

SKILLED SMILE

wrong with Isabella's blood, she could be in danger and I will be damned if I lose her.

Pressing my thumb on the scanner the private lift opened and I got inside it with the head of the laboratory scientist following me. "What's wrong?", I asked and his answer shocked me to the core.

"We couldn't figure out, doctor Waldorf, her blood is different as if she is not a human species", he said and I clenched my hands hard. My heart was pounding in my chest as I walked every step towards the laboratory, towards the microscope where they put her blood sample and gave one look to all the six technicians and they were equally freaked out as head scientist.

"We were discarding her blood sample after her reports came clean but then suddenly her blood sample fell in DSLOM -8 chemical accidentally and the colour of the blood changed into silver colour", he explained and I nodded my head grasping on everything he was saying.

Looking into the microscope I saw the structure of her blood and the DNA was not like a normal human should have but it looked as if RNA is surrounded by two DNA's and I frowned.

"Get me some LADP liquid", I ordered and they followed and when I dropped the liquid in her blood sample and put it in the speedol machine and waited for one minute which felt like years. As soon as the machine beeped my heart beat increased as I carried the test.

Smearing blood on the fresh glass slide I put that under the microscope and my eyes widened as I saw what it was. Her blood has huge number of antibodies than any normal human

SKILLED SMILE

and it has strongest structure that wouldn't let any antigens settle on it basically....Isabella's blood is cure for any kind of cancer and I honestly think it could be cure to any fucking disease ever existed or may breakout in the world.

"You all are signing Non negotiable contract and keep this between the walls of this fucking laboratory, do you understand?", I seethed and they all nodded.

Taking my phone out I called the only person I could trust in this matter.

"Hello, Mr Cruz Collins's assistant speaking, how can I help you?", a lady asked and I replied hastily.

"Tell your boss, Doctor Waldorf called and I requested a meeting fixed with him tonight ASAP at my place", with that I hung up the call.

"If I find any of you leaked this information.... I will hunt you down and fucking kill you", I warned them and walked out of the lab making sure they take my threat seriously because for Isabella's safety I can even kill anyone to everyone.

CHAPTER TWENTY EIGHT

ISABELLA'S POV

Rafael looked stressed throughout the journey to the carnival. As he was driving the car and I sat in the passenger seat beside him I couldn't speak much because of Lisa, nick and bruce who were glancing time to time at us weirdly.

Shrugging their look I gathered some courage as I put my hand on his and asked silently with my eyes. He smiled and it wasn't forced but loving. My heart felt relieved at his gesture and he held my hand and put it on the gear and drove us to the carnival and Lisa winked at me. I blushed shaking my head. It was a cute gesture but this woman finds dirty meaning in everything rafael does. Getting down the car I saw another car following us and I frowned. "They are for your security", he said and I huffed tiredly. He always thinks something will happen to me when he should be afraid something might happen to him, because he is world's famous surgeon.

"Let's take a look around before getting on rides", Lisa suggested adjusting her shorts and crop top and I smiled noticing they are wearing couple dress. His and her was written in cute font on their pink top and nick's t-shirts respectively.

I looked at rafael, he was wearing his expensive black jeans and white full sleeves t-shirt, pairing it with white sneakers. I would be lying if I tell he didn't make me feel butterflies in my stomach in every clothing he pulls but right now he looked too ethereal that I almost drooled.

"Did I tell you how beautiful you are looking today?", rafael asked and I blushed shaking my head hoping he didn't saw me checking him out.

"No? When was the last time I complimented you?", he asked and I pouted before answering. "Might be last night?", I sulked and he wrapped his arm around my waist before whispering in my ear, "You look so damn beautiful that I could eat you for….".

I cut him off smacking him on his chest and gasped, "Rafael! You are not supposed to say things like this here!".

He smirked raising his eyebrows and asked "I'm I supposed to say things like this when we are alone?".

"Ughh, stop it! Someone might hear us!", I whisper yelled but Lisa interrupted. "Too late, we heard everything already!", she sang and I turned red in embarrassment and rafael chuckled pecking my forehead.

"Come on lets go", bruce said rudely and I saw rafael clench his jaw. Holding his hand I smiled at him, "Doctor waldorf… let's find out who is courageous among us", I challenged and he smiled before telling.

"It's you, sweetheart, you are the strongest and courageous woman I have ever met in my life", hearing him say that my heart swelled with pride. Grinning at him I followed my friends into the spring carnival to spend another wonderful day of my life.

SKILLED SMILE

As we explored the place which was busy but beautiful I kept smiling widely as we passed through different stalls. Different types of food was being sold and accessories to games which were looking too fun. I stopped at a particular shop and bought bunny ears hair band one for me and one for rafael. "I'm not going to wear that!", nick complained looking at similar pair of ears which were in pink colour matching their outfit while the one I selected was white and it would go well with rafael's white t-shirt and his blue hoodie am wearing which reminded me of his blue eyes.

While Lisa and nick kept bickering about the headband I hesitantly showed what I bought to rafael. He smiled and without a word put his own as well as mine too and pinched my nose as he said, "Miss bunny, you look cute like this". I beamed, "Doctor bunny, you look cute too".

Lisa gestured towards rafael and elbowed nick in his stomach and he coughed before sighing heavily and accepted his defeat by wearing the band Lisa bought.

Later an hour passed by as we kept exploring the place. Slowly Lisa approached me from behind and I smiled at her. "Do you know your man is buying everything you saw twice?", she asked and my eyes widened as I turned behind to see rafael buying the brown teddy bear I saw on my way.

"Oh my god!", I gasped looking at two bodyguards who's hands are filled with almost everything I touched or saw in stores. I ran towards rafael to stop him from wasting so much money on things like this.

SKILLED SMILE

"Rafael! What are you doing?!", I questioned bewildered as he paid a stack of dollars for fifteen feet teddy bear. "Buying you everything you like", he said and I frowned shaking my head.

"No, you are buying everything I saw or touched", I retorted and he smiled innocently.

"That's same thing, hummingbird, you don't look twice at the things you don't like", he said and I dropped my jaw in shock.

"This is cutest thing I have ever seen a guy doing!", Lisa exclaimed clapping her hands and I sighed. Not her encouraging him on this! I cursed internally when the bodyguard almost stumbled carrying the teddy bear back to the car.

"Okay, that's enough, let's pick a ride", I said trying to divert rafael from shopping more.

"Hmmmm.... . This seems new", Lisa said pointing her finger towards a new ride in the carnival.

"That's disco pang pang, it was supposed to be ban in America because it's dangerous", rafael jumped immediately denying the ride.

"May be they started this year, it's thrilling to be honest, let's try", I said and received a deadly glare from rafael.

"You aren't riding that, hummingbird", rafael spoke without leaving space to fight. Wanting to be a brat again just to get on his nerves I smirked.

"You aren't stopping me, doctor waldorf, I will ride whatever I want to *ride,* if you are afraid you can stay here", I said pushing my curls off my shoulder and saw rafael's jaw clench.

SKILLED SMILE

"Woah! This would be so fun!", Lisa exclaimed clapping her hands and bruce stayed back telling he isn't interested when rafael paid extra to reserve whole ride just for us.

Lisa gushed at this and I rolled my eyes, "Asshole".

Lisa and Nick sat opposite to us while rafael and I sat beside each other and rafael already put his arm around my waist and I scowled slapping his hand off me.

"I'm not a little kid", I said with a glare and saw rafael exhale heavily trying to keep his cool.

Sitting comfortably on the seat holding the railing hard in my palms I counted 3.2.1 making myself ready before the ride started and when it did. I yelped and rafael's hand immediately held me in place and I gritted out. "Don't hold me! Am not a kid!".

"Fine!", he said through his gritted teeth and I rolled my eyes at his over protectiveness.

The ride picked up speed bouncing and rotating us and I laughed enjoying the ride, yelping and screaming in joy. Suddenly then lisa's hands left the railing and she ran other side of the ride as a headless chicken screaming and falling. Nick who tried to help his girlfriend slipped off the seat and held the railing with his one hand and twirled as a broken antenna screaming for help.

"Nick! Save me!", Lisa cried out as she ran towards nick's almost laying body and he cursed. "How the fuck do I save you! Am hanging in between life and death", he retorted and I laughed. I couldn't help. I laughed so hard that my body shook with laugher and my eyes teared up while rafael had a calm smile on his face looking at me enjoying the ride.

SKILLED SMILE

"Nick you are embarrassing me in front of doctor A.O.W.Y! Look how bella is laughing at us!", she complained and the ride suddenly stopped and jerked us in anticlockwise and Nick held railing with his two hands now sitting on the floor of the ride.

When the ride jumped in speed, Lisa ran towards Nick almost stepping on his man parts which almost gave Nick a heart attack.

"Oh my god! Fuck! You are going to destroy your means of pleasure, you fucking crazy woman!", he screamed in terror and I laughed more.

"I'm sorry, if I do destroy your hickory dickory cock.....but you have to trust me I will never trade you for another man or dildo!", Lisa assured him and I choked on my own laughter and it served me well.

My hands slipped off the railing and I fell on my knees right in front of rafael and held on his thighs to not slide off to another corner. "Oh my god!", I cried out and Lisa and Nick laughed their asses off this time.

"Karma is a real bitch, hummingbird!", Lisa yelled in happiness and Nick laughed more.

"Help me", I cried out holding tight on rafael's thick muscular thighs and he smirked. "You are not a kid, hummingbird", he mocked and I clenched my jaw. As ride bounced my face came *face to man parts* of rafael and I blushed in the darkest shade I ever did. As the ride kept bouncing, my face almost slammed into that area and rafael grunted.

"Fuck! I have imagined you in this position but not in this situation", he admitted and I bit my cheek to stop myself from asking something I will regret later.

"Oh my god!", I gasped as my lips almost touched him. "Please! Can't you see! My face is just above your man parts", I gritted out and he smirked.

"Man parts? Huh?", he asked and I blushed.

"Yes, now please help me get up!", I begged and he smirked tracing my lower lip with his thumb. This bastard could keep himself at place in this bouncy ride without much struggle and the reason of this strength is of course the time he spend in gym.

I couldn't count the number of times I peeped as a pervert while he worked out in gym and ogled his Greek god like body.

"I will help you on one condition", he said and I frowned.

"What?!", I squeaked and he smirked before he broke a bomb on me.

"Tell dick, cock and penis".

RAFAEL'S POV

Her eyes widened and her jaw dropped in shock and I chuckled internally. "I am asking you to pronounce various synonyms of man parts", I said shrugging my shoulders enjoying how bewildered she grew understanding I was indeed serious.

"No! You can't do this!", she whined and my eyes shone in amusement. If she is struggling to tell dick I wonder how embarrassed and shy she would be when I ask her to touch or hold it... doing something else is far out of picture.

The ride jerked and her hands slipped off my thighs and I immediately caught her arm with one hand and she yelped and sighed in relief. "We don't have whole day hummingbird, tell or am leaving you", I said and she looked back at stumbling Lisa and Nick and sighed.

"Okay......okay fine!", she groaned as she said.

"C...co.. Cock, d... dick and... and p.. Penis", she squeaked out her face as red as beetroot and hid her gaze from me.

I pulled her up and settled her on my lap and she gasped as she felt my hard girth on her ass through our jeans. Thank god that the ride didn't continued or else I would have fucking came in my pants with her ass bouncing on my dick.

CHAPTER TWENTY NINE

ISABELLA'S POV

"This place sells amazing churros", Lisa said pointing towards a cafe and I smiled excitedly. I have been avoiding rafael after that embarrassing moment in disco pang pang and he have been smirking as if he got world's best award. Bruce was walking beside me and I smiled at him holding his hand as we used to do always.

"Are you okay Bruce?", I asked and he sighed giving me a smile. "I am fine, just some…. weather change is hitting me off", he said and I nodded my head kicking the stones on my way.

"Oh god! The cafe is full, we need to get take out", Lisa said and rafael cleared his throat giving a sour look to bruce he walked away telling he will get our order.

I stood with Bruce, Lisa and Nick waiting for rafael to come back then bruce said something I never expected he would have something like this going on in his heart.

"Bella….. I can't stop myself from telling this, I love you, I really love you", as soon as those words escaped his mouth my eyes widened and Lisa and Nick gasped.

"Wh…", our words were cut off when a ear piercing sound rang and the balloon behind me blasted. People around us who were laughing and enjoying now started screaming in terror and running wildly. Another sound echoed and I screamed closing my eyes.

"Lisa!", Nick panicked holding his girlfriend tightly and tried to pull themselves away from the crowd almost walking over us.

"Hold my hand", bruce said as he tried to drag me along with him and I was so shocked and panicked that all I could do was search for rafael.

"Come!", bruce yelled dragging me out and we ran few steps and suddenly I fell on my knees and people kept pushing and walking over me. My hand slipped out of bruce's hand and he looked at me apologetically and I understood. *He left my hand because I was slowing him down.* Tears started flowing from my eyes and I cried in pain when people stepped on my palms and I braced myself on my knees and palms knowing very well that they will walk over me if I fall completely on the ground.

"Rafael!!!", I cried out and I saw people running away from me.

I am alone, everyone left me, am alone…

Only those words rang in my head and my breathing turned heavy. I blinked my eyes and saw through blurry sight, rafael was running towards me. Everything besides him turned blurred and I saw rafael in slow motion. Pushing people off his way, he made his way towards me. I cried. As soon as he reached he fell on his knees covering my body with his and I sighed in his chest catching my breathe as tears kept flowing from my eyes. His expression was mortified as he laid his eyes on me and the next second he ordered.

"ROUND UP!".

Nearly twenty people rounded us in their black bodyguard suits and I hid myself in rafael's arms.

"Shh, am here, no one is going to hurt you", he said and his voice came out strained.

Lifting me in his arms he hugged me close to his body and I hid my face in his neck greedily taking his scent in my lungs trying to assure myself I am not alone. Rafael came for me. He wouldn't leave me.

Placing me in the car as bodyguards kept walking close to us we made it safely and rafael got inside the car beside me.

One of the bodyguard got in the driver's seat and another in the passenger seat beside him and I was shivering in fear. "Shh, rockstar! You are safe now", rafael cooed and I looked into his blue worried eyes.

"I thought I was alone", I said and my lip quivered as I sobbed. "It was my fault, I shouldn't have left you in the first place", he blamed himself hugging me tightly and the car took off.

"Your hands are injured", he said looking at them and I winced when he held them. "We will get them cleaned as soon as we reach home", he said and I nodded my head.

When we reached home the guards escorted us inside the mansion and rafael gently laid me on the couch. Anastasia gasped looking at my freaked out condition and ran towards us with a medical kit and a bowl of clean water.

SKILLED SMILE

"How did this happen?", Anastasia asked and I frowned shaking my head. "Someone attacked her in the carnival, I should have been more careful", rafael said taking cotton and cleaning my scratches on my palms and knuckles.

"Oh my god!", Anastasia gasped covering her face and I winced when rafael put ointment on my injuries and wrapped a bandage on them.

"Mr Collins was waiting for you in your office", Anastasia said and I frowned.

"Take Isabella to my room", he ordered and I shook my head.

"I won't, I will stay with you eden, please ", I begged as more tears fell from my eyes.

He closed his eyes before pressing his lips on my forehead. "I am here, I won't be going anywhere, it's a important meeting, please, lay on the bed and watch your favourite anime while you eat something", he said and I shook my head vigorously.

"How about we take some cheesecake and I will accompany you until Doctor waldorf comes back?", Anastasia suggested and I sighed.

"Promise me you will be back soon", I said showing him my little finger and he connected his own with mine with a smile and said, "I promise".

Waiting for rafael for two long hours he didn't come yet and I grew restless.

"Bella, he is in his office, he didn't leave mansion, you should stop worrying", Anastasia cooed lovingly as she sat beside me and the anime running on the TV was long gone as a background video for our chitchats.

"I saw a huge teddy bear in your room, that guard said doctor rafael bought it for you, in fact everything you glanced at", she said with a teasing smile and I blushed smiling and nodded my head.

"Rockstar, we need to talk", rafael said as soon as he came inside the room

~

RAFAEL'S POV

"I heard what happened in the carnival", Cruz said as soon as I entered the office. I sighed.

"Gio said this will happen, someone ordered a hit on her", I said sitting on the couch in front of Cruz.

Cruz nodded his head understandingly and I offered him a drink which he politely denied telling he won't drink this soon. "So what is that you needed me again?", he asked and I ran fingers through my hair.

"Before I tell this, you should know that I trust you, you did a huge favour by saving me and my career legally proving I wasn't the reason behind those deaths and now... this is something bigger I am trusting you with", I said and his lips twitched in a smile.

"That's my job, rafael, where as you save people, I save innocent people", he said and I nodded my head.

"Isabella Miller – her blood is cure for cancer and not only that, I believe it's cure for every single disease known or will be known in human existence", I said and his eyes widened slowly understanding what I said.

"Is this possible?", he asked and I gulped hard.

"My scientists found that her blood turned silver in lab when it accidentally mixed up with a solution and when I looked into it her DNA was different than normal DNA as if she is not naturally born but someone human made", I said and my throat turned dry.

"So you want to carry the experiment and want legal documents?", he asked and my eyes grew bewildered before I shook my head.

"Fuck! No! I want my scientists to sign non negotiable contract and want legal papers telling no one has right to use Isabella in any way to clear their doubt about her blood and exploit her", I said with finality in my words and this time he smiled.

"You love her?", he questioned and this time I smiled.

"Something like that", I replied pressing my lips together.

"Rafael! Fuck it! Rafael!", Gio yelled storming into my office and both Cruz and I stood with a scowl on our faces.

"Gio... you can't storm in my office like this", I gritted out and he shook his head turning the TV on and put the news channel and my knees buckled and I sat back on the couch.

"Isabella is Anabella's twin sister?! And Robert Davis's granddaughter?!", Cruz said in disbelief and I frowned.

"Her details were different in her certificates, her birthday was in damn January eleven while Anabella's was on July fourteen!", I reasoned and Gio nodded his head towards the television.

"He is announcing her existence to the world, telling his granddaughter was targeted in a carnival and he wants her safety and it's only possible when she is with him and if am not wrong he also mentioned about the innovation he is going to announce when his lovely granddaughter comes back to him", he said rolling his eyes and I clenched my jaw in anger.

My whole body vibrated with wrath as I know what that bastard could do for his own benefit and Isabella don't deserve all of these.

"We need to save her from him, Gio I need you to increase the security around the home and if possible book a plane ticket for Isabella and no one should ever know where she is", I said and he nodded his head.

"We will send her to my private island", he said and I nodded my head.

"I will keep the papers ready", Cruz said then asked. "By the way where is carter?".

"Carter is out of city, they are opening branch in L.A", I said and they both nodded their head understandingly.

"You need to tell everything you know to Isabella, trust me rafael, truth from a stranger hurts more than lies from our loved ones", Cruz advised giving a brotherly pat on my shoulder and I nodded my head realizing it's time.

CHAPTER THIRTY

ISABELLA'S POV

"I will be going to check if the doors are locked", Anastasia said clearing her throat and walked out of rafael's room and I sighed.

"What's wrong rafael? You look like as if you have seen a ghost", I joke and he smiled shaking his head.

Coming close to me he sat beside me on the bed facing me and took my bandaged hand in his as he said, "I want you to trust me, rockstar, as eden, not rafael".

I frowned. "I trust you as rafael too", I said and he exhaled heavily.

"There is something you should know because... its your right", he said and I could practically feel my heartbeat thundering in my chest. Is this the time where he tells he isn't obsessed with me and found another new obsession and tell me get the fuck out of his life? But for a reason I know the way he look is.....as if he is in love with me but it could be my hallucination because that's what I wanted to see?!

"I am listening and I trust you", I said and his hold on my palm tightened, not too hurtful but tight enough that I couldn't pull my hand off his.

"Annabella Davis..... Was the woman I trusted and she changed the vaccine that should be given to those people", he said and I nodded my head slowly sinking everything in my head.

It's Anabella... so who was she that rafael trusted her so much?

"She was my professor, Doctor Robert Davis's granddaughter and... and... she is your twin sister – which I found out just now", he said and I sucked in huge amount of air and exhaled.

"Oh my god!", I said placing my other hand on my heart and shook my head before telling, "I'm so sorry behalf of my sister, rafael".

He laughed humourlessly and said. "I thought it's her ghost when I saw you for the first time eating ice cream with bruce because she was supposed to be dead, she fell from a building and died in front of me", he said and tears streamed down my eyes. Is it painful that I found it was my sister who betrayed rafael or it's more painful that she was dead?

"Since I believed she is dead, I thought I was seeing things but you were real and I even dug her grave up to find her but no – she wasn't in her grave where we all buried her with honour", he told and I gaped placing my hand on my mouth. She isn't dead? It was too much to wrap my mind around all these things. How am I supposed to react to this truth which was bitter than any other lie that could break people's hearts.

SKILLED SMILE

"Then I thought it's you, that you are Annabella and you changed your look from blonde hair to these beautiful red curls", he said wrapping my stray hair around his finger. So all this obsession was because he thought I am my sister? But then it hit me. He said he was mistaken and I smiled internally. He didn't wanted me because I was Annabella he wanted me because I am Isabella.

"Rafael... why did you trust her?". I felt dumb asking that question but I needed to know what happened between Annabella and rafael and why he trusted her with his life time hard work. Even though I know what was coming, I just wanted to hear it from him.

"Because I thought she was love of my life", he said and I found my heart shattering in pieces.

"But she wasn't, she wasn't someone as important as you are to me Isabella, for you I can kill people remorselessly", he said and I shook my head. "You are a doctor, promise me, you won't kill anyone", I said and he smiled promising.

"I promise but if it comes to save you or the world I will save you", he said and his voice held a promise which made me shiver. Is something wrong?

"Then you understood am not her?", I asked changing the subject and he nodded his head wiping my tears away.

"Where is my twin sister now?", I asked and he shook his head.

"We don't know".

Even though knowing that Annabella and rafael had some past which could be deeper than the present we have I was happy, why? Because I know am not alone, I have a family, I don't know if they know it and want me but I hope they want me. Even if they are bad, they are my family.

"It's okay, I understand and honestly I feel happy that I have a family", I said smiling but that didn't last much.

"There is something more I needed to tell you", he said his voice strained and heavy when he breathed out.

"You are not safe here, am sending you to private island of one of my trust worthy friend and you will be staying there until I think things are safe here for you", he said and I shook my head laughing humourlessly.

"I'm not going anywhere without you, rafael", I declared through my gritted teeth because I know I couldn't live without him.

SKILLED SMILE

CHAPTER THIRTY ONE

RAFAEL'S POV

"I will come now and then to meet you, rockstar", I said trying to convince her and she pushed my hand off and glared at me.

"I don't want to go anywhere!", she screamed at me and my heart clenched.

"I don't want to go anywhere away from you, without you, rafael", she screamed choking on her cries.

I stood on my legs and turned the television on before I said, "Look at that man".

Isabella flinched at harsh tone and got off bed wiping her tears which didn't stop flowing. My heart pained for her but she needed to see this. She needs to face reality of the family she thinks she is lucky to have. She could be happiest person because she found that her blood, her family is alive but she have to understand that the same family threw her away from their lives. The video of her grandfather's interview played in front of her eyes and her eyes widened.

"That man is your so called grandfather, who knew you were alive all these years but he never showed up, do you have any idea why? And do you know the sensational invention in medical science he is talking about here is *you* damn it!", I yelled at her and she jumped in fear because of the tone of my voice as well as the harsh truth.

"Your blood is cure for fucking all diseases that a mankind will ever see!", I added, her eyes widened and her hands flew to her mouth.

"If you want to live rest of your life as a fucking rat whom he will use to experiment in his laboratory then stay here or else leave, I don't know about you but I can't see you like that because I love you! Am fucking obsessed with loving you!", I admitted and I heard her gasp. Then her cries hit my ears after she said, "I love you too".

She covered her mouth and cried, "I love you too, that I know I couldn't breathe without you, rafael, I will die, if you let your hummingbird free – she will die".

She said and my eyes softened and my heart swelled in happiness. Isabella loves me and all I hear is that she loves me in my ears again and again.

"What did you tell?", I asked in happiness while she hid her face in her palms crying her eyes out.

"Please tell it again", I asked wrapping my arms around her and she slowly peeked through her hands as she said.

"I love you, I love you rafael and I love the way you love me", she said and I smiled widely. Her face was flushed and her eyes were swollen. Her freckles were looking enchanting on her flawless skin.

"I love you so much, I love you so fucking much", I said and smashed my lips on hers.

I couldn't think. The kiss was so emotional with all the love she is putting in it and I was a greedy bastard I wanted every last drop of her love. Holding the back of her neck I pulled her closer to me and kissed as I was sealing the promise to keep her safe. To keep her mine. To stay hers for forever.

"Ah", she moaned when I sucked on her tongue. Shoving my tongue inside her mouth I devoured her. Her breathing increased and I know she needed to breathe and I gave her a moment by leaving her lips and kiss her neck. Taking my time I pressed on the sweet spot and she moaned and gasped at the sensation holding my t-shirt tightly in her palms and I sucked on various parts of her neck leaving the darkest shades of hickeys with my palms resting on her ass.

Primal need to devour her completely, to make her mine got in my head. Fuck! As if that has ever left my head from the day she came into my life. I want her, I want her everything but I will wait for her. I almost chuckled at how embarrassed she was telling cock and what my intentions are....., they will be too overwhelming for her.

We both were breathless when I stopped and her lips were bright red with the torture she put them through to stop moaning and I traced my thumb over them and she sighed.

Her eyes closed and her red curls sprawled over her face she looked like a goddess. Her face tear stained and the freckles covered cute nose and cheeks was something I would never get tired looking at. Innumerable nights I spent counting them before I fell asleep peacefully without any dreams that haunted me.

"Eden", she breathed out opening her eyes which were now dilated just as mine but the dark brown colour of them made her look as a bambi eyes of a doll.

"I want you, please", she begged and I felt my cock twitch in my pants.

"It's okay, you need to rest now", I said pushing her hair away and she shook her head.

"I need you, eden, please", she whispered and I was in a no condition to defy her plea.

I kissed her. Hard, passionately, hungrily and devoured her mouth taking my time with her plump rose petal like lips and she moaned in my mouth with need.

Lifting her up in my arms I laid her on bed still kissing her lips and neck as far as I could with my hoodie on her.

Taking hoodie off her I eyed the goddess beneath me. With her reddened cheeks and nose she shut her eyes tightly while she covered herself with her hands in embarrassment which she shouldn't be. Not in front of me.

"You are fucking beautiful", I whispered in her ear taking her hands off her and she shivered. Goosebumps peppered her skin with my breathe on her stomach and I slowly made my way to

SKILLED SMILE

the valley of her breasts. Taking off her white bra off her body I kissed her lips once again and she moaned.

My rockstar loves kisses.

I smirked when she tried to cover her moans by biting her lip as I massaged her blossoms which were fucking perfect in my hands.

"Don't hide your beautiful moans from me, rockstar, you don't need to be embarrassed, those drive me fucking crazy and I swear to God I will be making you scream some good sinful sounds throughout the night", I said blowing on her pink pebbles and she shivered as a whimper left her mouth.

I did same with the other one before drawing circles around her perky pebble with my tongue not giving her the satisfaction by sucking on them yet and she grew restless.

"Ahhh, eden!", she whined with her fingers threaded between by hair as she tried to push my mouth where she needs.

I chuckled, "Impatient are we now, rockstar? Do you have any idea how many times I have imagined you like this? How many times I have fucked my hand thinking about how would your pussy taste?", I whispered in her ear and she gasped.

"Please", she begged and I smirked.

Slowly I pulled her jeans down with her wet panties and I was goner just with the view if her pink dripping pussy crowned with perfectly red trimmed hair.

"fuck! You are so beautiful, everything about you is so beautiful", I said pressing my lips on her thighs leaving hickeys on my way to her welcoming sweetness.

When I reached her warmth I looked up at her and her eyes were tightly shut. "Look at me, rockstar", I said against her core and her breathing increased and her chest rose and fell beautifully.

"Look at me rockstar, look at me claiming you in every possible way", I said and her eyes opened slowly and she peered into mine. Asking her silently, question of consent with my eyes she smiled shyly nodding her head.

"Relax, don't strain your muscles", I said running my fingers on her thighs and parted her legs wide and put them on my shoulders before diving into her heat which burned all the past pleasurable memories for me. If this is what they tell too much of anything can kill you, am ready to fucking die eating the nectar of her pussy.

As a hungry animal I licked a long stride of her wetness and she gasped and moaned and my cock was dying to be free to taste the sweetness I found.

"You taste so fucking sweet", I grunted and started eating her out as if it was my last meal.

Her eyes rolled back and her fingers dug in my hair and she clenched her hands fisting my hair.

Fuck!

I grunted in the pleasurable pain she is providing while I increased my speed.

I hummed against her clit, licking it, biting it playfully before I dug my tongue deep in her cunt. she screamed and mewled tightening her hold on me.

SKILLED SMILE

"Eden!!!", she gasped when I fucked her with my tongue and my thumb went straight to her clit and rubbed it as I applied her own juices on it. Her breathing accelerated and her eyes rolled back and seeing her come apart like this became my favourite part of making love to her.

"Fuck! Come in my mouth rockstar, just like that", I said fastening movements of my tongue and she came. Screaming my name from her lungs fighting to catch her breathe she came apart underneath me and I licked off her come humming to its sweetness and hovered over her capturing her lips in a deep kiss.

"Taste yourself, how fucking sweet you taste... another reason to be obsessed with you", I said kissing her madly and she moaned at taste of her and my fingers reached her slit parting her lower lips for entrance.

Gathering her juices I smudged them on her clit and stimulated it with fast moments of my thumb and she moaned in my mouth and slowly I slid one finger in her cunt and I felt like my breathe got caught in my lungs. "You are so fucking tight", I groaned in her mouth and started pumping my finger in her slowly and increased the pace eventually dragging another orgasm from her. If she is this tight around my finger there is no way she could take my cock.

Licking her throat to her perky nipple and finally gave her what she wanted. I latched on them sucking them and drawing sinful melodious sounds from her for which I am officially whipped.

"Eden!", she moaned as I bit on it and did same with her other blossom. Perfect round and just enjoy big to fit in my hands they were made for me. She was made for me.

Still pumping my finger, I slowly pushed another one when I thought she is enough stretched. The wet sounds of her pussy her moans, heavy breathing filled in the darkness of the room with moon light peeping through the balcony and this moment became more intense with our confessions.

I can't and will never have this in other way. Clenching around my fingers she came once again screaming my name as a fucking prayer and I sucked on her juices off my finger and pulled my T-shirt off my body and threw is somewhere before taking off my jeans along my boxers letting my cock free.

"Look at me", I ordered and her eyes opened and her face glowed with post orgasm effect and she looked as a fucking goddess of heavens like this and I was ready to worship her in every fucking possible way.

Pumping my cock few times I smeared my pre cum from the slit and on the head of my cock and her eyes followed my movements.

Gulping hardly she blushed before saying, "There is no way that's going to fit".

I smirked. "What's *that* rockstar?", I asked and she blushed hard again.

"Man parts?", I asked and she groaned cutely hiding her face in her palms and I chuckled.

Hovering over her I smiled pressing a sweet passionate kiss on her lips and she kissed me back with same passion holding my jaw with her bandaged palms.

SKILLED SMILE

"Are you sure? We can stop now if you want", I said asking another time if she is ready for this.

Taking her hands off her face she smiled and nodded her head, "I want this, I want you, I want this only with you".

I kissed her, slowly trying to keep her attention on the kiss and smiled between in the kiss when she said, "Please".

Kissing her sweet spot now and then while I kept kissing her I rubbed the red of my cock on her clit and she buckled her hips up.

"Uh, please, eden", she moaned and I lined my cock at her slit gathering her juices and coated my cock with it before slowly easing it inside her. Her tightness made me gasp and my breathing hastened as I tried to control myself and Isabella yelped in pain and I stopped going inside her.

"I'm so sorry, rockstar but this pain will soon fade away", I grunted nuzzling my face in her neck and she exhaled heavily taking sometime and eased herself and I pushed whole length inside her when she spread her legs wider and raised her hips. After making sure she is adjusted to my size.

"Ahhh, eden", she moaned scratching my back with her nails and I grunted in pleasure before I started thrusting in her tight cunt slowly which made me see fucking stars.

"Oh fuck!", I grunted when her pussy kept clenching and unclenching around my cock and she screamed.

"Please don't stop, this feels so good", she moaned as I increased the pace before I said.

"I swear to God, I won't be stopping until your legs keep shaking".

With that I increased my pace holding her nape of the neck and kissed her breathlessly and our strained breathe mixed with each other's and I kept her eyes locked with mine as I kept thrusting in her drawing another orgasm from her. She screamed my name again and this time her orgasm gushed out on my cock and my balls soaked in her squirt juices and that made my cock grew harder.

"Fuck! You are doing so good", I said as I increased my pace in her wet cunt and the room is filled with my grunts, her mewls and moans and wet sounds of our bodies colliding with each other.

"Ahh, Eden", she moaned again at the feeling of her orgasm building up and this time I rubbed her clit with my thumb and soon she came along me taking my thick ropes of cum in her and my body collapsed on her.

Catching our breathes we stayed like that before I got off her and pressed a kiss on her lips and forehead.

"Let's get you cleaned up", I said and she shook her head in denial.

I chuckled. "This is the first and last time am being gentle on you, next time I won't stop until you made mess on the whole fucking bed and we have to sleep in other room".

"Ugh, don't talk like that", she groaned hiding her face in my neck and I chuckled.

SKILLED SMILE

"Does it makes you uncomfortable?", I asked trying to know if she finds it that way but she meekly denied and said. "No, it makes me let you do everything you tell".

I smiled. *My freaky girl.*

"Good night, Eden", she whispered dozing off and I kissed her hair.

"Dream good, *my hummingbird*".

CHAPTER THIRTY TWO

ISABELLA'S POV

My body felt sore, every part of my body made me whine in pain. I stretched my arms and slowly opened my eyes. The side of my bed was empty and I was naked in duvet and last night memories hit me and I almost teared up thinking rafael regretted last night.

But then cold air hit my body from the balcony and I turned to look rafael standing shirtless wearing his jeans from last night which was hanging low. Getting up from the bed I winced. Bed was stained with blood and I bit my lip. Gulping hardly I covered myself with duvet and walked towards rafael ignoring stinging pain between my legs and thighs.

"Rafael", I called him and my voice came out sore and I cleared my throat. As he turned his head to see me and his face was tense and that made me fear about whatever running in his head.

"Rockstar, why did you wake up this early?", he asked looking at the clock which read six a.m.

SKILLED SMILE

"I felt cold", I admitted as he pushed my hair behind my shoulder and kissed my forehead and I sighed in relief.

"Rockstar... I don't want us to be like this", he said and my heart dropped in my stomach.

He is indeed regretting last night.

I clenched duvet hard in my hand and bit my cheek to stop myself from crying but then he got down on his one knee taking a box and opened it to reveal most beautiful ring I have ever seen.

"Marry me", he said and I cried ugly big tears covering my mouth.

"You scared me when you said you... you don't want us to be like this", I complained and he got up immediately embracing me in a hug.

Pressing my face on his naked chest I cried hitting him.

"Oh goodness, No, I didn't mean that, am sorry if it came out like that", he apologized kissing my lips as I kept crying.

"I hate you", I said smacking him on his chest and he chuckled.

"I love you too, rockstar and you know that am not a very patient man, now tell me will you marry me and make me the happiest man on this earth", he said and I smiled wiping my tears as he kissed my forehead then eyes.

"I will marry you, Doctor Waldorf".

SKILLED SMILE

He grinned capturing my lips in a passionate kiss after putting the ring on my finger and I almost moaned when he squeezed my ass.

"Aren't you sore?", he asked and I blushed nodding my head.

"Then we should stop before I fuck you again", he grunted and I bit my lip trying to stop myself from saying something he would tease the hell out of me for forever.

"Now... let's get you cleaned up and feed you something before making you Mrs Waldorf", he said lifting me up in his arms and I yelped.

My eyes widened and I asked, "This soon?".

"Fuck ,yes! I have been roaming with that ring in my pocket since your birthday and planning the wedding since you shared your dream wedding when we were in Paris", he revealed and I smiled widely.

"Doctor Waldorf... then why didn't you propose me on my birthday?", I asked smirking and he winked at me.

"Well I would have if you liked me proposing you on your birthday party after getting caught by jerking off imagining you", he said and I threw my head back and laughed.

"I thought you were in problem, sick or something so I barged into your room to help you but I swear I didn't see anything", I said honestly and he pretended as if he was dropping me on my ass and I gasped clinging on him tightly.

"I was definitely in a problem... just like now and I guess this time I need your help", he said putting me down in the shower and yanked duvet off leaving me naked in his marks from last night.

Turning the shower on for me, he took his pants off and joined me in the shower and I helped him as he requested with his *man parts*.

CHAPTER THIRTY THREE

ISABELLA'S POV

I would be lying if I said I wouldn't be laughing when someone said that I will be marrying today. After the attack in carnival, after rafael said I have some special blood that could heal any disease, my grandfather announced my existence and asked for my safety by warning people who planned the attack and rafael telling he *thought* he was in love with my twin sister.

Now all my dreams made sense. Eden was real, the blonde me was real but she wasn't me but my twin sister and that means the man who used to torture me should be real along with the voice which called me a failed project – my grandfather was obviously real.

A shiver ran through my spine as I thought about that chair which rafael said could probably was used for electric shock and said I need not worry about anything anymore because now, he knows from whom he should save me and how.

"You are looking beautiful, I bet doctor A.O.W.Y will come in his pants seeing you walking down the aisle", Lisa commented and my eyes widened and I smacked her head playfully.

Owing she smirked and said, "Mrs Waldorf is so protective of her soon to be husband…. Just like him", she said and I rolled my eyes.

"Did you hear anything from bruce?", I asked and Lisa sighed shaking her head.

"No, he said to Nick that he is ashamed of what he did and in fact I think he should be, nick and I would have never left when we knew he was going to leave you alone in fucking crowd to be smashed down under people's shoes", she gritted out and I winced.

My phone beeped gaining my attention and I sighed unlocking it just to see text message from Bruce.

From: Bruce

I won't ask for your forgiveness because I know I don't deserve it, I wanted to tell you… you are free to break my promise, rafael deserves to hear the song you wrote, not me. Have an amazing life ahead, I know rafael will make sure you do.

Your best friend.

A lone tear slipped through my eyes and I wiped it immediately locking the phone. I didn't have heart to reply and I didn't. If he loved me, he should have been honest with his feelings at the beginning and if this is how our friendship ends… I will

SKILLED SMILE

remember the good memories and forget the bad ones and it will eventually take time.

"Look! Media is waiting for your entry! They are going crazy to know who Doctor Waldorf is marrying and they are all over the yacht in helicopters", Lisa exclaimed and I smiled shaking my head.

"I swear to God, I will jump in the ocean to catch the bouquet but you are my bestie right you should throw it in my way", she pleaded and I smiled.

"Of course I will make sure I do", I said and she grinned widely hugging me.

"Thank you, thank you, thank you", she chanted and I smiled.

We heard a knock on our door and we broke the hug as Lisa fixed my dress one last time.

It is a beautiful Cinderella gown in sky blue colour and rafael is wearing navy blue suit and sky blue tie to match with me. Holding the white roses bouquet I walked towards the door looking my steps as I was wearing tallest heels I have ever did in my life. Hopefully I won't fall down. Nick promised he won't let me fall which I doubt he won't but am not going to tell this to his face.

After all he is the brother I never had, the time we shared our food, played video games and hid desserts all of those memories of us together which I will cherish my whole life along this one.

"You are looking beautiful", nick complimented and I smiled.

"Thank you, so do you look beautiful", I said and he scoffed.

SKILLED SMILE

"Handsome, it's handsome", he corrected and I grinned when Lisa smacked on his head hard.

"It's her wedding and brides don't like to be corrected on their wedding day", she scolded and he pouted rubbing his head before smiling at me.

"Doctor A.O.W.Y is waiting for you impatiently, let's go", he said locking my arm with his and I smiled exhaling heavily.

"Let's go", I said and we walked towards the stage which was decorated with white roses and everyone was wearing the dress code rafael made sure to add in the invitation. The yacht was decorated with lights as it was almost eight p.m. and the starts were decorating the sky with moon smiling at us. The waves brought a cool breeze which warmed my soul. Everything was perfect just as I dreamed it would be.

Most of the people here were the one I don't recognize. Two I do is Carter – rafael's best friend and the tattooed man who I met twice. Anastasia and Lisa became my flower girls and I was happy that they wanted to.

Carter smiled at me widely when the tattooed man winked at me playfully and rafael sent him a glare which made me smile.

My possessive doctor.

Rafael was looking as amazing as he always do and today if it was possible he looked better than always.

His dark black hair styled back and his electric blue eyes pierced into my soul taking my breathe away. His gaze travelled from my head to toe as if he was looking through my dress and his eyes dilated.

I gulped when nick handed my hand over to rafael and his warm and huge palm held mine before he pressed a kiss on it.

"You are looking breath-taking, rockstar", he said and I smiled before telling.

"You are looking as perfect as you always do Eden".

He grinned. Walking to the centre of the stage he announced, "Meet my fiancee Miss Isabella Miller".

Everyone smiled and clapped their hands and rafael draped his arm on my waist pulling me closer to him as he read his vows when priest asked.

"I, Rafael Eden Waldorf – take you, Isabella Miller as my lawfully wedded wife, with your faults and your strengths, as I offer myself to you with my faults and my strengths. I will help you when you need help and turn to you when I need help. I choose you as the person with whom I will spend my life".

I blinked my eyes to get rid of tears as I said mine.

"I, Isabella Miller – take you, Rafael Eden Waldorf as my lawfully wedded husband, with your faults and your strengths, as I offer myself to you with my faults and my strengths. I will help you when you need help and turn to you when I need help. I choose you as the person with whom I will spend my life".

"Now you may kiss the bride", the priest announced and the yacht erupted with claps and hooting, encouraging our new

SKILLED SMILE

beginning as they showered their blessings on us which would keep us far away from any disasters. I smiled widely when Rafael grinned as he said, "I was waiting to kiss you since morning, it's been ten hours and forty eight minutes I kissed you last time".

"Stop counting the wasted time, doctor waldorf and kiss me", I whispered earning a smirk from him before my husband kissed me. Passionately he kissed my lips knowing he own my soul now – which was always his. The promise to protect it with his everything poured into me and a lone tear escaped in happiness and I kissed him back, promising him love he deserves through out his life.

RAFAEL'S POV

Breaking the kiss I pecked her forehead and lift her chin up as I gestured her to the sky and the firecrackers erupted lightening the dark sky in silver and blue colours and *my wife* gasped covering her mouth and her eyes twinkled as innocent kids eyes. Indeed she is as innocent as a kid and her heart is purer than anything or anyone's I have ever seen or met.

"This is amazing rafael, I love it", she cooed and I smiled widely.

"And I love you", I said and kissed away her tears.

"This is the last time am letting you cry on little things like this Mrs Waldorf. From now on you will only cry when my cock is deep inside your pussy and am fucking your brains out", I whispered and she mewled making me smirk.

"Sorry to interrupt newly wedded couple but my assistant said she wanted to give *merida* something", Cruz said interrupting our talk.

I smiled hearing she comparing my hummingbird to a Disney Princess and Isabella beamed.

"This is Mr. Cruz Collins and she is his assistant Miss Stella Correale", I introduced and Stella dragged my wife away from me and Cruz sighed.

"Don't worry she won't kill your wife, she is just excited to see red head just like her", he said and I frowned.

"But her hair is black with purple highlights? Yes, she dyed them but she is redhead", he said and I smirked.

"You slept with your assistant, wasn't that in your not to do list?", I asked as we took a glass of champagne from the table and he sighed.

"Well... I slept with her first then she happened to be my assistant", he said glancing at her.

"How do you know you love Isabella?", he asked and I exhaled sipping my champagne.

"I just know by seeing into her eyes, if she smiles – my heart beats so fast that I couldn't breathe, if she cries – my heart beats so fast that I couldn't breathe", I said smiling looking at her how she quickly became comfortable in stella's company.

"So basically we can't live when we are in love?", Cruz asked and I shook my head still looking at my wife as I answered.

"Anyone can live but you would die for your love".

~

SKILLED SMILE

"Rafael! You will break something", my sweet innocent wife squeaked when I carried her on my shoulder in the darkness of the mansion.

"The only thing I want to break tonight is your tight little pussy", I said and received a smack on my ass.

"Did you just smack me?!", I fake gasped and she chuckled doing it again.

"If you talk things like that I will", she threatened and I bit her ass playfully on her bare skin as I removed her wedding gown in living room on my way to our wedding chamber which Anastasia decorated even I told her not to.

The whole floor was covered with rose petals and the room was illuminated with candles and the bed was draped with clean white sheets. Throwing Isabella on the bed gently and she bounced and giggled making me smile.

"So Mrs Waldorf, didn't you miss me today?", I asked and she smirked shaking her head.

"Hmm so I think last night wasn't enough to make my humming bird miss me", I said taking off my tie, belt and threw my shirt in the corner while I got on the bed.

"You are so fucking beautiful", I said and she blushed licking her lips. Those pouty lips that were wrapped around my cock in the shower today morning as she sucked life out if me played in my head whole day and now she is laying beneath me as my fucking wife.

SKILLED SMILE

"I want to try something with you tonight", I whispered in her ear and her breathing increased.

"Do you trust me?", I asked and she nodded her head before whispering.

"Yes".

"My good girl".

"What would be the word you use when it gets too much for you?", I asked running my fingers on her curves and admired her in her black lace lingerie.

"Blue", she whispered and I smiled knowing very well that she choose that word because of my eye colour.

I blindfolded her eyes with my blue tie and kissed her lips then her jaw and her neck and goose bumps peppered her skin.

Lifting her hands up over her head I bonded them together then hooked it with the bed post.

Licking her ear lobe I whispered, "Welcome to a hell of a ride".

CHAPTER THIRTY FOUR

ISABELLA'S POV

I couldn't move my hands nor I can see. Honestly being this helpless is making me wetter than I already was. Every touch on my body...I feel it in my core. Rafael teased me with small touches. His fingers skimmed over my skin and I shivered. Slowly he removed my bra and my panties by keeping his touch on my body and my breathing accelerated.

"How do you feel, rockstar?", my husband asked and I mewled when he barely touched my nipples.

"Please, touch me", I begged struggling underneath him and he chuckled putting my whole body on fire.

"I will touch you... but not yet", he said while I heard opening and closing of the bed side drawer.

"What is it?", I asked when I felt something cold on my clit and gulped.

"It's a vibrator, have you ever used it before?", he asked and I blushed shaking my head.

"N.. No", I answered and it came out strained because right now I am needy. Needy for my husband to fuck me.

"Hmm… so I better start slow", he said and my body jolted up when the vibrator was placed on my clit and it made me scream.

"Ahhhhh, eden", I cried out in immense pleasure as I felt myself on some peak I thought I would never reach.

"Let's make something clear okay, tonight or whenever you are tied to bed, you will be calling me Doctor Waldorf, you have no fucking idea how it turns me on", he said and increased the speed of the vibrator.

I squeezed my legs trying to close them and rafael smacked on my pussy and I yelped.

"Owie… that hurts", I cried out and he spoke.

"You can always use your safe word, rockstar and everything will stop".

I shook my head, though this hurts this is good kind of pain which would make your toes curl your breathe hitch and body shake with pleasure. I think I this kind of pain – this feels so ecstatic.

"Doctor Waldorf…", I cried out as I almost reached my orgasm but everything stopped.

"Ughh", I grunted and rafael's fingers went straight between my legs and his fingers gathered my wetness and he brought those to my lips and I opened my mouth immediately.

Sucking off his fingers as he taught me morning I hummed and I felt him smirk against my ear.

"Fucking sweet right?", he whispered and I nodded my head.

"Please Doctor Rafael, I want you", I begged shamelessly and I felt him taking his pants off.

"Tell me what you want from me, rockstar", he asked as he aligned his cock to my pussy.

Teasing with its head at my opening he smacked with it on my clit and I bit my lip hard before telling.

"I want you to fuck me!", I squeaked out and he pushed his one or two inches not giving me his everything he asked.

"Fuck you with what?", I blushed. But that didn't stop me from telling my husband what I want.

"I want you to fuck me with your cock, Doctor Waldorf", I screamed as he pushed his whole length in my pussy and I yanked my hands off from the bondage to touch him but it was of no use.

Trusting into me powerfully sending me on the edge just in few pumps he asked, "You want to touch your husband?". I nodded my head as I mewled and whispered.

"Please I want to touch you", I cried and in a second my hands was free after my blind fold was off.

I wrapped my arms around my husband who was fucking me hard and strong that with every thrust I felt the bed shake and my body jerked upwards.

"Ahhhh, eden", I moaned as I came and suddenly he turned on my stomach and lifted my hips up before putting his cock back inside and my eyes rolled back as he kept pounding in me from behind. Massaging my breast with his one hand he pinched my nipple and I moaned.

"Ahhhh, this feels so good", I cried out and he grunted.

"Yeah, my hummingbird likes this? Like to be fucked hard by her husband", he asked his words strained and sexy and I nodded my head vigorously before telling.

"Yes! Oh yes! Uhmmmm", my breathing became heavy as I came again and this time rafael came along me and his warm liquid filled me and I signed at the ecstatic feeling.

When he pulled his cock out I laid on my stomach and felt cum dripping out from me and pushing it back with his fingers and a weird sound escaped from my pussy and I hit my face in pillow and groaned in embarrassment remembering how Lisa used to rant about her *this* problem and how she feel un sexy doing it and said most men don't like this happening to their woman.

"You don't need to be embarrassed about it rockstar, it's normal, it is called queefing and it happens when air escapes through your vagina", he explained and I slowly peaked at him.

"Aren't you like grossed out?", I asked and he frowned shaking his head.

"I'm serious, rockstar, it's normal, I was the one who pumped it in you, there is no way I would be mad or grossed about it", he said and smirked.

SKILLED SMILE

"In fact it fucking turns me on that I made your pussy sing", he told and I blushed hard hiding my face.

"Can you feel your legs hummingbird?", my husband asked and I frowned and nodded my head confused.

"Yes, I can feel them".

Flipping me on my back he grinned pumping his already hard cock as he said, "Then we are not done yet".

I smirked spreading my legs.

If my husband is ready to take me on a hell of a ride, I will ride him to hell and back.

CHAPTER THIRTY FIVE

ISABELLA'S POV

Yawning I rubbed my eyes before opening them. I smiled when my eyes fell on the note rafael left on the bedside table.

My hummingbird,

Don't skip your breakfast

I made your favourite pancakes today

XOXO ;)

I smiled brightly covering my naked body with duvet as I heard knock on the door. "I will be there in few minutes", I yelled knowing it's Anastasia double checking on me to wake me up for breakfast. Twenty days of being Mrs Waldorf could be amazing if and only if you don't have to eat all three meals on time.

Sighing I brushed my teeth, tracing the purple marks my husband left last night and blushed when I thought about how he surprise me every time.

Shaking my head to get rid of those thoughts I got into shower and took a quick bath and went down after making sure am looking presentable – not fucked with all the marks.

"You are looking beautiful, red is doctor rafael's favourite colour", Anastasia said smiling widely at my red floral frock with yellow flowers on them.

"I will be going to the hospital afternoon", I said beaming at the breakfast placed on the table.

I drooled over the salty and sweet breakfast and gulped it down as fast as I could because that was tastiest food I ever ate.

Rubbing my tummy in delight I wiped my mouth and Anastasia ruffled my hair happily.

"I want to cook rafael's favourite food too", I said and Anastasia chuckled.

"It's your kitchen Mrs Waldorf, you don't need to ask me", she said and rested my hands on hips giving her a cute glare.

"I barely cook, you are the one who keeps this place hygienic and cook for us, it *is your* kitchen", I said and her eyes softened.

~

After packing the food which I made and Anastasia helped me in chopping telling that rafael will kill her if he found out I did everything myself. I got in the car with two bodyguards in it along with ben.

"Good afternoon Mrs Waldorf", they said bowing politely and I smiled.

"To the hospital please", I requested and they nodded their head professionally and drove me to my husband's hospital.

SKILLED SMILE

~

"Mrs Waldorf… good afternoon", the receptionist greeted and I smiled at her greeting her back.

"Good afternoon, is Doctor Waldorf in his cabin?", I asked standing near the reception and she checked her iPad before replying.

"He is currently doing daily check ups of patients, you can wait for him in his cabin", she suggested politely and I smiled nodding my head.

"Thank you".

Taking elevator I reached second top floor of the building and went straight to my husband's office and my eyes widened as I saw the person sitting on his chair.

"What are you doing here?!", I ordered anger seeping through my body as he smirked wickedly.

"This is how my lovely grand daughter greets me?", he asked and I winced hearing him call me his grand daughter.

"I remember what kind of human you are, a person like you can never be my grand father", I snapped while I clenched my free hand.

Getting up from his chair he walked towards me and backed off from him and he smirked.

SKILLED SMILE

"Do you know your mother used to have same hair like you and your father had blonde hair just like Annabella", he said and I bit my cheek trying not to listen anything he was saying.

"Your parents always wanted you both sisters make name in medical world but I had better plans", he said and I felt my eyes get blurry.

"The blood running in your veins is my invention", he said as he raised his hand to touch me but suddenly the door snapped open and my husband's fist collided with the monster who claim to be my grandfather.

"Don't you dare touch *my wife*", rafael seethed landing punch after punch on him and he coughed blood. I turned my head immediately not wanting to see and closed my eyes when my grandfather warned.

"You stayed a step forward by marrying my grand daughter, you won't be always ahead, once I get my hands on her – you can't do anything", he gritted out and I cried.

"Get this bastard out of my building", rafael ordered and I saw security dragging him out and rafael immediately wrapped his arms around me.

"Are you okay, rockstar?", he asked and I sighed in his chest and nodded my head.

"I don't know how he broke into my office, we need to get this placed checked before touching anything", rafael said and I nodded my head silently tearing up.

"Come on, let's go to the pent house", rafael said lifting me up in his arms and carried me to the top floor if the building which has laboratory and pent house.

"Are you okay?", rafael asked and I smiled handing him the empty glass of water.

"I brought your favourite food", I said and his eyes brightened and he pressed his lips on my forehead.

"You didn't have to rockstar", he said and I rolled my eyes and served us the cioppino and steamed rice and he nodded his head impressed before talking a spoonful of soup and tasted it before groaning.

"This is the best cioppino I have ever tasted", he said and started stuffing his mouth and I smiled proudly.

When I took a spoonful of soup my stomach twisted. I frowned taking another spoonful of soup and rafael almost finished his bowl and I drank some water when he eyed me worriedly.

"Are you okay rockstar?", I smiled nodding my head and took another spoonful of soup and everything kicked out.

Covering my mouth I ran into the nearest washroom and emptied everything. Rafael followed me totally freaked out and held my hair up and kept rubbing my back when I emptied my stomach in toilet bowl.

Tears rolled down my eyes at bitter feeling in my mouth. "I don't feel good", I choked out and rafael tensed. "It's okay, relax", he said and after I thought it's over he helped me get up and brush my teeth.

SKILLED SMILE

"My mouth tastes bitter", I choked out wiping my tears as he helped me get out of the red dress I was wearing.

"It's okay rockstar I will give your favourite chocolates", he said and my mood immediately brightened.

Munching on the chocolate I sighed and rafael checked my temperature. "You have mild fever", he said and I frowned shaking my head.

"I won't take medicines for this", I fought and he glared at me and I matched his glare.

"Fine, if you won't eat these...", he said smirking and took his stethoscope and tied my hand together and I gulped.

"I will eat you out until you get tired of coming on my mouth and agree to take those pills", he said and my breathe hitched.

Taking his shirt off my body he pulled my panties down and I leaned back on the couch.

"Play with my hair, you can even fucking pull them but keep your hands together, can you do that for me rockstar?", he asked and I nodded my head hesitantly but the wetness in between my legs grew more and more with every passing second.

Taking a long lick of my slick opening rafael hummed and I gasped at the intensity this man makes me feel every single time.

Kneeling in front of me he devoured my wetness as if it's the only thing that could satisfy his thirst and I kept chanting his name as if he is the only word I know and indeed Rafael Eden Waldorf is written all over my soul, my heart and every inch of

SKILLED SMILE

my body, on every breathe I take… he is in it and without him – his hummingbird couldn't live.

"Ahh, eden", I moaned as he thrust his tongue inside me and I clutched his dark black hair in my palms at the intensity he was providing while his tongue fucked me and his thumb drew circles over my clit. I was already sore from last night and this… this feels so good. My eyes rolled back when I felt my orgasm build and my thighs shook as I came hard screaming my husband's name.

"Oh my god", I cried out when he didn't stop pushing his finger inside he licked my clit gathering my come on his finger before shoving them into my mouth and I hummed cleaning them off as his pleasurable torture was on my clit. He blew warm air on my core and I shivered.

"Look how sweet you taste, rockstar, I won't stop eating you out until you are too tired to get up and eat the damn pills", he said and I mewled.

"Please eden", I said and he hummed against my core as he lapped all my come as well as wetness before generating heat in my body again by juddering my clit with his thumb and I screamed.

"Ahhh", my core pulsed as I spammed all over his mouth and he smirked wiping his mouth with the sleeve of his black shirt as he licked me clean again.

"That was amazing, can you do that again?", he asked and my shocked expression made him smirk.

"You will do it again", he said fastening his speed on my clit and I was too tired and my pussy was swollen.

"Please, eden, I will take the pill, please stop", I pleaded and everything stopped.

"Here", he said handing me pill and I glared at him before swallowing and decided to take my revenge someday.

CHAPTER THIRTY SIX

RAFAEL'S POV

"Everything is wrapped up?", I asked my PA and he checked my schedule one last time before telling. "Yes, Doctor Waldorf, everything is done".

I nodded my head, "Then I will be leaving early today", I said and went into my cabin which was well checked last day after that bastard left.

Taking off my lab coat I threw it on the chair and the door opened and I smiled widely watching Isabella pouting.

"What made Mrs Waldorf mad now?", I asked pulling her on the table and she gasped and smirked before tracing her thumb on my lower lip.

I groaned grabbing her ass and whispered, "You are getting feisty day by day Mrs Waldorf, can I know what happened to my shy and sweet little innocent wife?", I asked before kissing her neck and she moaned.

"Ah, Rafael".

I pushed her away, my hummingbird never moans my first name saying she likes Eden better. I immediately took four steps back and glared, "What the fuck are you doing here Annabella?".

She pouted and I wanted to puke, her hair is now dyed into fiery red just like Isabella's and her face is sprinkled with fake freckles she probably made out of make up and I gritted my teeth.

"I see you didn't miss me... but I did", Annabella said getting off the table and walked towards me and I looked down at her.

"You were dead", I said and looked into her eyes which weren't anything like Isabella. These eyes are cold, lack of emotions and cunning.

"I was forced to be... I never wanted to be dead, I never wanted to leave you Rafael but I had to, there wasn't any option", she said and I narrowed my eyes on her.

"It's funny how you think you were forced to do something you like – oops, love, you love deceiving people and you did", I said coldly and her eyes darkened.

"Why the fuck you are here?", I questioned sternly and she smirked.

"I came here to tell you... I will be staying with you now, you can forget about Isabella", she said and my jaw clenched in anger.

"If you think I will leave Isabella then you are fucking wrong Annabella because one can live without a soul but cannot live without a heart and *she is my heart and I can sell my soul to keep her with me*", I said through my gritted teeth and her hands clenched as she walked towards me.

"I'm so sorry for you Doctor Waldorf but... if you couldn't be mine, I won't let you be someone else's", saying that she jumped on me with a injection in her hand and I twisted her hand pressing her on the wall and whispered in her ear after putting the injection near her neck ready to pierce it through her skin.

"You might be mistaken my love for your twin sister Annabella but for her I can fucking kill anyone, even you", I gritted out and she struggled to free herself but all of it went in vain.

"If you want me to leave you now... tell me everything you know, from what happened to Isabella in the orphanage and why her blood is different".

She took a deep breathe as she calmed down and whispered. "She isn't the only tortured soul Rafael, I am too but I am designed in this way", she said and I frowned.

"My grandfather wanted to create sensation in medical science and after our parents died he had legal rights on me and Isabella", she said and took a deep breathe.

"We were six when we were thrown in laboratory as fucking animals to be experimented and my grandfather wanted to make us into humanoids", she said and I frowned.

"I have so many active neurons in my brain that I remember anything I see once and Isabella was supposed to be like me", she said and I clenched my jaw.

"We were locked in white bright rooms and given electric shock to stimulate our brain cells along with medication which were particularly designed for it and my body accepted the procedure but Isabella's denied, so she was punished by giving too much electric shock that she would forget everything from last day... even her name", she revealed and my heart clenched in pain for my wife.

"But later with her tests we found that her blood should cure every possible disease and to carry the experiment my grandfather wants her now, at any cost", she told and I let her free pushing her on the floor and discarded the solution in the syringe and threw it in the Dustbin.

"What was the reason to change the vaccines which were given to the thirty seven cancer patients?", I demanded and she answered without missing the beat.

"We Davis are gods in medical field and only we have right to inventory that will change fortune of people...we couldn't have you as our competition", she said and I scoffed folding my hands.

Medical science isn't competition, it's a team work. Team work of doctors to make this world a better place which sometimes God couldn't do. We are supposed to strive together for the humanity sake but I guess money indeed makes people compete.

But that would go up through their heads because all they think about their power which comes with money. It's okay, not all people study to save lives but to make their own life even if they had to take others and the life Annabella and Robert have ahead wouldn't be their favourite and I will make sure of that.

"Your date of births? Why are they different when you both are twins?", I asked one last question before I do what is necessary.

"She almost died on January eleven because of extreme shock and that one injection changed her whole DNA structure so grandfather made sure his project J11, should be always a reminder", I winced. I couldn't help. Everything Isabella went through made her delicate I wouldn't say week. Everything Annabella went through made her a psycho who wouldn't show remorse about her actions.

"Do you regret?", I asked and a cunning smirk plastered on her face.

"I regret not marrying you when you asked me to be your wife", her words mocked and I smiled.

"Thank you for showing me I deserve better", said that door of my office snapped open and cops entered through it dragging Annabella away. Her eyes widened and she started screaming and struggling in their hold but she knows she is in trouble with finger prints of her on the last vaccine batch I could prove Annabella was the one who changed a actually working medicine.

I sighed rubbing my eyes. Everything Isabella went through was heavy on my heart and I will make sure to give her the best life she deserves ahead.

~

"Hello", I answered the phone as I was driving back to the mansion, to my wife.

"Rafael! It was Annabella who ordered hit on Isabella, Robert wants Isabella alive just for her blood and when he gets that he is going to kiss Isabella and put act of showing Annabella is dead", Gio said and I frowned.

"Didn't they make everyone believe Annabella is dead?", I asked and he sighed before telling.

"Who Annabella? Rafael, that woman you got arrested....she returned as red head shows it's your wife Rafael, either way they will kill your wife or get her arrested life time in Annabella's place", he said and the grip on my steering tightened and I pressed brakes immediately moving my car to the side.

Hanging up the call with Gio I answered Robert's video call just to see my Isabella tied to a electric chair and crying her eyes out.

CHAPTER THIRTY SEVEN

RAFAEL'S POV

"I will fucking kill you bastard, if you lay a single finger on my wife", I growled. Isabella's tears streamed down her face more when Robert put a knife to her stomach and she started shaking her head as no while her mouth was gagged. Anger and helpless made my whole body shake and I clenched the phone in my hand tightly when Robert said.

"I thought it would be a waste of time killing my project J11 to save my humanoid but thank you rafael you made it possible that even if I kill her the J11 project will be alive and for that I just have to postpone my little red head – Isabella's death for nine months", he said and I froze. My eyes widened at what he was instating.

"Don't you dare hurt my wife!", I yelled and punched the car and the gun safe opened revealing a gun and a spare phone. I secretly texted Gio to track the number am speaking to so that I can reach wife before he hurt her and *my baby*. My child.

"You want to talk one last time with your husband? Tell him that you are pregnant with your own mouth? Huh?", he asked yanking her curly red hair back and she sobbed.

"Okay I will give you one second", he said taking her gag off.

"Rafael!!!!", my wife sobbed choking on her tears.

"Rockstar... don't cry, I will save you, no one will hurt you, I won't let anyone hurt you", I said as a lone tear of frustration and helplessness escaped my eye and I pushed them away clenching my jaw. Sitting in that chair would be traumatic to her specially when she have nightmares about it all the time.

"I will come to save you", I said and she replied.

"Chocolate, my favourite chocolate", before her eyes closed.

"Isabella!!! Isabella!!!", I yelled panicking and my heart clenched in pain when Robert said.

"Don't worry Doctor waldorf, I gave your wife safe anaesthesia, you know before we start the process to make her forget you, this will be easier task if we have to keep her for nine months", he said and my whole body burned in rage.

Before I tell anything he disconnected the call and I received Gio's call.

"I'm sorry man, we couldn't track the number as call was short", he said as soon as I answered the call.

I exhaled and a hope boomed in heart when I remembered what my wife said.

Her favourite chocolates.

She gave me a hint where she is.

Though with all the fear running in my veins I smiled.

"I know where she is gio, where all of these started".

~

The place was all covered in rust and the building was burnt and gio and I coughed as we walked inside. "This place smells like shit", he said and I nodded my head.

"Because people died in this building", I said and his eyes widened.

"People were burned down here?!", he gasped and I smirked.

"Don't tell me you fear ghosts", I taunted as we both walked towards the area which was supposed to be red area of the building.

"Shhh", I said as I heard shuffling of steel instruments in the corridor and gio alerted.

I told him I can go all by myself but he said he wanted to help his friend which I suppose a favour in debt so that he could come back to me to get his illegal wounds stitched.

"They are here", he whispered and I nodded my head.

"Okay so they are only four members and one among them should be your wife, we can easily take them down", he said and I nodded my head.

"There is another door from that room there", I gestured to the place where I used to sit and talk to Isabella when she was locked in.

"Let's go", I said and he followed me silently without making a noise.

Slowly peeking into the door we saw Isabella passed out on the chair and Robert wearing a white lab coat ordering something to his team of two people.

"It's better you go through that window and reach Isabella when I barge into this room", he said and I nodded my head.

Walking towards the window without making a sound I slowly jumped inside and gio barged inside through the door pointing his gun at Robert and their eyes widened. I took their moment of shock as a chance and rushed towards my wife and tried to free her as fast as I could.

"Rockstar", I cooed trying to wake her up but she was past asleep. "Gio we want that old bastard alive", I yelled and gio shot the remaining two on their arms and legs while he kept Robert in head lock.

"How the fuck did you find us", Robert grunted coughing in gio's tight hold and I smiled taking my wife in my arms realizing along with her right now am lifting my baby too. Our baby.

SKILLED SMILE

"Guess you wouldn't find out because you don't have any favourite chocolate......", I said and gio finished.

"...... eating place".

"I never thought it would be this easy", gio sulked and I laughed.

"Well, James Bond, this is not your book, this was mine, my fight with my obsession to fall in love", I said pressing a kiss on my wife's forehead lovingly.

EPILOGUE

THREE YEARS LATER

ISABELLA'S POV

"Mommy look! Daddy bought me a crown", my two years old daughter said running towards me and I smiled widely welcoming her in my arms.

"Oh my god this looks beautiful", I cooed and her eyes twinkled and I awed at them how beautiful she looks with her dad's eyes.

If Rafael's eyes was my favourite, hope's eyes are my favourite among them though they are exactly like Rafael's. While he tells her curly red fiery orangish hair is his favourite because those are just like mine. Basically our daughter is mini version of us and I couldn't be happier having her other way.

"Hope, you should never run away from daddy like that", my husband tries to discipline her but she looked at him as if he had spoken some alien language.

"But daddy I didn't run, I flew", she debated putting her hands on her hips and I bit my lip trying to hide my laugh.

"Baby... we are humans we walk and run, birds fly", he said and her brows furrowed.

"Who said we are humans daddy? Don't you call mommy hummingbird? She is a bird which makes me a bird and we fly", she said smiling brightly as she spread her hands animatedly and ran around as if she is flying.

Rafael smiled shaking his head as he sat on the picnic blanket beside me and I grinned. "She is growing too soon, am not liking it", he whined and I kissing his cheek as I leaned into his chest holding my guitar. Looking at the Eiffel Tower and the beautiful rainbow on the lake, I sighed. how our lives have been changed and changed for good. Annabella and Robert are in jail and they will be throughout their life which Cruz made sure of. Gio is having his adventurous life and get back to Rafael with his *illegal wounds* which my husband likes to call and Carter is dating Bruce and that shocked the hell out of me. They are even so serious about their relationship that they are thinking about getting married this year. Lisa and Nick are enjoying their honeymoon as they dropped their one year old son at their parents and they were so happy to take care of him and here I am with the man who kidnapped me, brought me to the same city on our first date and gave the world to me by being in my life and I couldn't thank enough to God for giving me a beautiful daughter as hope.

SKILLED SMILE

"Rafael", I whispered and he hummed keeping his eyes on our daughter too afraid that she will get hurt in the time he blinks his eyes.

"Don't you think we are living a perfect life?", I asked and his lips stretched into a perfect smile.

"With you and hope in my life, it is, it is perfect", he said and I beamed.

"I want others to have a perfect life too...I want you to make vaccine with my blood and before you deny, I trust you", I said in one single breath and he sighed.

"You know I don't like to use you as a rat in lab experiment", he said and I grinned.

"Who said I am a rat daddy? I am a hummingbird", I said smirking.

He rolled his eyes cursing under his breath, "Only one ml of blood", he said and I smiled widely as he agreed.

"Thank you so much!", I exclaimed hugging him and he hugged me back telling, "I love you".

"I am obsessed with loving you", I said and he chuckled ruffling my hair.

"Mommy can you please sing me daddy's favourite song you wrote?", hope requested crawling on the picnic blanket towards us and I smiled.

"Of course baby", I cooed and Rafael took our daughter over his shoulders and she sat there comfortably holding her dad's black hair as support which Rafael don't mind.

Looking at *my family* which I craved to have I blinked my eyes trying to hide my happy tears and I sang while playing my guitar.

Don't leave me in the room of brightness

When you are in darkness

I couldn't survive here all alone

Night is cold

Am all alone

Then you showed up to light the bonfire of hope

When I woke up from my warm dream you weren't there anymore

Don't you see, you belong to me

Stop the hide and seek and come back to me

I couldn't breathe

Am sinking deep

No it's not because you took my wings

Because you were my wings

Now without you am losing hope to live

Freedom without you wasn't what I knew

Please take me back in your cage

SKILLED SMILE

Where I know you will keep your this hummingbird safe

From the storms of days and nights

You always shine in my eyes

Like rainbows and stars in the sky

Wiping my tears my husband whispered as my daughter clapped her hands in joy.

"Obsession made you my biggest weakness and love… love made you my greatest strength and I am obsessed with loving you Mrs Isabella Waldorf".

Sealing his words I pressed my lips to his falling into his obsession so I could fly in his love.

♫♩♪ THE END ♩♪♫

ABOUT AUTHOR

Well I exist but one day I won't but then you can feel me in my books:)

But if you want to find me...

INSTAGRAM: @author.skilledsmile

YOUTUBE: @authorskilledsmile

TWITTER: @skilledsmile1

the author, nor be otherwise circulated in any other form or binding or cover other than that in which it is published.

SKILLED SMILE